To my family…

For showing me, and teaching me, what love is.

PREFACE

I killed him. It was as if I had pulled the trigger myself. If only I had just stayed put. His only instruction had been to stay in the barn. I wasn't supposed to leave. I was supposed to wait for him there. If I had just done what he had asked me to do, he would still be here.

There was blood everywhere. I couldn't tell where it was coming from. Was I bleeding? I didn't feel any pain… The blood was seeping all over the floor. My now shredded dress was no longer silver and blue; instead it was the color of his blood.

"How do I make it stop? The bleeding won't stop…" I kept thinking over and over again. My hands were pressing on the wound but that didn't seem to be helping.

I couldn't wrap my mind around what had just happened. This couldn't be real. This was a nightmare. This was my nightmare. Everything had been taken from me. My life had been stolen. It was all my fault...

AUGUST

I looked in the mirror. I was stalling. Going downstairs only meant that the day had to start. I wasn't ready. I didn't want to listen to the good luck speeches. I didn't want to listen to Hallie talk about how excited she was. Of course she was excited. People loved her. It didn't hurt that she inherited our family's Scandinavian traits; round face, blond hair, blue eyes. She didn't just attract boys though, she attracted everyone.

I wasn't going to be able to put this off much longer. "Let's just get this over with," I said to my reflection.

I wasn't the first person to ever have to move. People moved all the time. It wasn't like I was leaving behind boatloads of friends. Things were just easier in Chicago. It was easy to be ignored in a school as large as mine. In a class of more than a thousand, no one had the incentive to care what I did one way or the other. Things would be different in Wabash.

Indiana. Of all the places my parents decided to move to, they picked the smallest town in a state made up entirely of corn. Dad thought that Hallie and I might benefit from some fresh air. What he really meant was that Hallie would benefit from space between her and her new friends.

It was my senior year and I would be attending Wabash High School. There were going to be 96 people in my class. There was no doubt that everyone in my class had known each other since birth. Families in a town like Wabash tended to plant themselves there. No one ever left. I was going to be the intruder, the new girl. There was no way to hide from it. I guessed that we were probably the first family to move to Wabash in decades, possibly centuries. There wasn't much draw to come to Wabash, other than the fact that it was the first electrically lit city. I wondered if anyone actually thought that was a big deal.

Our house in Wabash was bigger than the townhouse we had in Chicago. In Wabash I would have my own bedroom. It was painted the same color as Pepto Bismol and there were white frilly curtains that hung all the way down to the floor, but that didn't matter. I had never had my own room before. It wasn't exactly my taste of décor, but Dad promised that we could redecorate as soon as his practice was up and ready to go. The bedroom did have one amazing redeeming factor; it had a fabulous window seat that looked out onto the two acres of land that made up our backyard. The view wasn't glamorous, but it was better than nothing.

Dad was a dentist, so his plan was to open up a new practice in town. He picked the best possible location, directly across the street from the school. It wasn't like he was going to pop into school or anything, it was just the fact that he was going to be there and everyone was going to know it. Again, my goal was to be ignored, not pointed out.

Dad was like Hallie, he didn't get me. He didn't understand why I would want to be left alone. Why wouldn't I want to shake hands with everyone on the first day and introduce myself? Why not just wear a name badge saying, "Hello My Name Is…"? That was what Dad would do. He would walk up to strangers and just start talking as if he had known them all his life. Sometimes they would walk away immediately, but other times they would allow him to join in the conversation. Either way, he was happy just to have someone to talk to. I think he would talk to a chair if he thought it would listen.

Mom wasn't as bad as Dad, but she wasn't like me either. Mom was the type that had to make everyone around her happy. If that meant she was staying up until midnight baking pies, then so be it. She would do whatever it took to please the masses. I did not suffer from that problem.

My goal for tomorrow, my first day of school at Wabash High School, would be to survive. If I could just make it through the day, then the day would be a success

* * * * * * * * * * * * * * * *

The biggest perk to moving was Dad buying me a car. It was a used purple station wagon, but that was fine with me. As long as it got me to where I needed to go, I was okay with it. Hallie was mortified. She wanted nothing to do with the wagon. I couldn't believe she threw such a fit over a free car. To me the wagon equaled a level of freedom I had not yet been allowed to experience.

As I pulled into the school parking lot I could feel the tension forming. The sweat attack started. My heart was pounding. My stomach was immediately disagreeing with my breakfast. I felt like a lead blanket was being draped over me.

Hallie, of course, bounded out of the car and bounced into the building. She looked just right. Her hair was pulled back into a ponytail that swung with each step. She had chosen the perfect jeans that matched the perfect sweater. Her talent for making outfits slapped me in the face as I reviewed what I was wearing. My plain, straight, brown hair was being held back by a plain, brown headband. The old jeans I chose matched the old sweatshirt I had decided on. No makeup. No frills. I had decided at a young age that to me comfort was way more important than glamour.

Walking into the school was like walking into a foreign country. I didn't speak "farm." I saw kids walking around with their thumbs painted green. I had never seen so many beat-up trucks in one parking lot before. The school dress code seemed to be jeans and flannel shirts. I began to feel better about my outfit of choice.

I walked directly to the main office. Hallie, obviously, had already been there for her list of classes so that she wouldn't have to admit out loud that I was her sister. It didn't take long for me to get my class schedule. It was pretty straightforward, no big surprises. The school was tiny, only two hallways. I didn't foresee any major problems in finding my way around. In Chicago I had classes in six different buildings. I could definitely handle two hallways.

The one class I hadn't expected was gym. I didn't mind having gym, but it would have been better to not have gym. Evidentially everyone was required to take one elective each year. Gym was the only option that would fit my schedule. I was pretty good at sports, although I much preferred individual sports to anything involving teams.

I wondered what Hallie got. I would've loved to see her in gym. She could create fabulous outfits, but her athletic ability was nil. Having gym together would drive her crazy because for one hour every day I would be better than her.

The first half of the day was alright. It was the first day of school for everyone, so it wasn't like I was coming in the middle of the year. No one seemed to notice, or care, that I was there. Everyone already had their groups of friends. It helped that none of the teachers had seating charts so I was able to sit where I wanted; back row, back corner. Perfect.

Next came lunch. Hands down the scariest part of the day. The cafeteria wasn't in the high school. I had to walk across the campus and into the middle school in order to get food. Forget that. Note to self: bring lunch.

Walking into the cafeteria was how I identified who belonged in what group. The school was ridiculously stereotypical. There were the jocks and the cheerleaders, the people who chose not to shower, the farmers... So, where to sit? Hallie had magically found her way to the only table full of beautiful people; the only table where no one appeared to be wearing any type of flannel clothing. Looking at the table was like watching a toothpaste commercial. Everyone was smiling and having a great time all the while looking fabulous. No surprise, she didn't even glance in my direction; still pretending I didn't exist.

It wasn't that I didn't want friends; it was just that I didn't like the process of finding them. Dad always said that we have to make an effort to meet people; that no one will seek us out. I hoped he was wrong. Otherwise, I was sunk. I didn't have it in me, I wasn't the out-going type.

I ended up grabbing an apple and a sandwich and taking them with me back over to the high school. I sat down in the doorway of my next class and ate my lunch. It was so quiet.

I was alone. It felt different this time. In Chicago there were always people sitting alone on benches either doing their homework or reading a book. Here it seemed like everyone had a spot, as if being alone wasn't allowed.

Usually I felt like it was my choice to be by myself. This time I felt pushed out, forced away. Unwanted. Like I was a ghost. At least my plan of being ignored was working. Although, I wasn't sure if that was what I wanted anymore.

It was last hour. There were definite pros and cons to that. The day was almost over, good news. I had to go to gym, bad news. The gym smelled like sweaty boys and dirty socks. It made me wonder how long it had been since the floor was cleaned. Surely there was a deodorizer available that could kill the odor.

Mr. Roberts was the gym teacher. I sort of got the impression that he was also the coach for every sport the school was involved with. The staff of the building was so small that no one else had time, or wanted, to bother with extracurricular sporting activities.

"You must be Sidney." He was holding a clipboard and checking off names as students walked in.

"Yep." Easy questions got easy answers.

"We aren't dressing for the first day. Go ahead and have a seat on the bleachers. We will get started in a minute." Mr. Roberts was really young. He looked like he could have been one of us. I didn't find him attractive, but it was clear that a lot of the girls did from the way they were mooning over him. I hoped for his sake that's all it ever amounted to.

"Welcome to gym. This shouldn't be new information for most of you." I was almost disappointed to see that Hallie was not going to be spending last hour with me. "Bring appropriate gym wear everyday. This class will be included as part of the practices for track. So be prepared to run."

Good news, I could run. I wasn't going out for the Olympics or anything, but I could handle the mile, no problem. I heard a lot of groans from the kids around me. I didn't care. I was relieved to know that this class was not going to be based around dodging flying balls or hitting various objects with a bat.

True to the rumor, he let us out a few minutes early. I got to the wagon as quickly as I could without bursting into a run. I had to wait for Hallie, but that was okay. Once in the car I was safe. No one could see me. Hear me. Ignore me. Hallie came a few minutes later after breaking away from her new group of friends. She ducked into the car and we were off.

* * * * * * * * * * * * * * * *

"School went okay?" Mom knew that Hallie would already be on the list for prom queen while I would be lucky if I had spoken to more than one or two people.

"Sure. The Earth didn't crack in half or anything." I tried to sound okay, but Mom knew. She always did. I didn't feel like talking about it. Suffer in silence. "Do you care if I go exploring? I wouldn't mind getting to know my new environment a bit better."

"That's great. Just be back before it gets too late."

This was the freedom I wanted. I just needed to breathe. I didn't want to listen to Hallie talking about how great school was and I didn't want to hear Dad lecture me about being more outgoing. I just wanted to… escape from my reality. Pretend for awhile that I wasn't stuck here; that I could go anywhere and do anything.

I got in my car and just started driving. It didn't matter to where, I just drove. I was driving down county roads; roads labeled with numbers instead of names. Pavement turned into loose gravel. I was glad the corn had already been harvested, otherwise it would have been like driving through a tunnel. I was gone for an hour before I made the discovery. I didn't know how I got there; how I found it. I just ended up at an unexpected but very welcomed waterfront. The road just sort of stopped where the water started. I got out of the car and walked to the bank. The body of water was small. I could have easily swum to the other side. Its size didn't matter. Seeing it gave me a sense of peace.

Thanks to my own personal fashion sense I was able to sit on the ground without the fear of ruining my outfit. This was my new spot. My new special place.

I sat there until it got dark. I didn't want to leave. There were no worries here. No family. No locker room. No cafeteria. Here I didn't have to worry about what my hair looked like or how dorky my clothes were. There was no one to impress. No one to hide from. I didn't have to worry about what to say or not to say. It was easy for me to understand why people became hermits.

I took my time driving back home. It was only seven. No one would start to worry for awhile. I tried to find something good on the radio but only found bluegrass country and "Classic Oldies." Note to self: make CD for car. Being an older wagon, it didn't have a plug-in for my iPod.

I chose to drive in silence so I could think of answers to the inquiries I knew I would get upon arriving home. Dad would have a gazillion questions and then a lengthy lecture to follow about the importance of meeting new friends and making good impressions. He would fully expect me to just sit there and listen without adding any input. Really, that was okay because providing any input only created the risk of adding another additional segment to the already unabridged version of his lecture. Definitely not worth it.

Sure enough upon coming home, "Where did you go? See anything interesting? Figure out all the hot spots in town?"

"Sure thing Dad." I didn't want them to know that I was sitting alone for hours and I didn't want to tell them about my discovery. I had decided on a "no intruders" policy. I didn't feel like sharing anything just yet.

"Hallie said that school was wonderful. Did you get the same impression?" Here we go... probing for information.

"It was okay for the first day. I am sure tomorrow will be better."

"You know, first impressions are important. They forge the path for new friendships and social contacts that could someday be invaluable..." At that point I tuned him out. There was no point in continuing to listen to a speech that I had already heard. I would just nod my head from time to time and throw in a "right" and "okay" as I saw fit. As long as the illusion was there, he would just keep on going. His longest run ever was two straight hours.

"Sidney didn't talk to anyone! She just sat there like a lump all day. Did you even eat lunch, or were you afraid of the cafeteria?" Hallie asked as she entered the living room. She just had to join in. What did it matter to her how I spent my day at school? I went to all my classes and I survived without any major traumatic events. That in itself made the day a triumph.

"Yes. I ate lunch…" I looked at Dad who seemed to be gearing up for another lecture. "I just go at a different pace than you, that's all. I like to feel my way around first. "

"Yeah, that's what you are doing." Hallie laughed and plopped down on the couch.

"Girls, stop." Mom was almost as non-confrontational as me. "Hallie, I am very glad that you had a good day. And Sidney, I hope that tomorrow is better. I am sure that if you make an effort you will meet plenty of nice people." I did appreciate that Mom tried to understand, but clearly she didn't.

It didn't matter to me if I became popular or not. All I cared about was surviving. I had to make it through one year. After that, I was out.

Between Dad's lecture, Hallie's attack, and Mom's attempt to help I was officially maxed out. Thank God I had my own room.

I went upstairs to my still pink room and pulled out my journal. I planted myself on my bed and started writing. Writing in my journal was my way of venting. I allowed myself to blame everyone else for all of my problems. I screamed at my dad on paper for uprooting me out of my comfortable life. I cut off Hallie's hair. I put blue dye in her shampoo. I washed the toilet with her toothbrush. I hugged my mom. I cried on her shoulder. I let her in. I told her how much it hurt today sitting by myself in the hallway. In my journal I wasn't afraid to speak my mind. I had opinions that mattered. In my journal I wrote down the story of my alter ego.

When finished writing I tore out all of the pages and ripped them to shreds. I never left evidence of anything I wrote. I didn't want to risk anyone else's eyes reading what I had written down. My writing was just for me.

I laid down and shut my eyes. Tomorrow would be another day. I took a deep breath. Just survive… One year….

SEPTEMBER

Over the next few weeks I was able to find a new routine. Wake up. Go to school. Go to the beach (for the lack of a better word). Go home. Go to bed. That was my life. Hallie had managed to find someone, some girl named Emmie, who would come and pick her up every day before school. Emmie had a much more acceptable mode of transportation. I guess anything was better than the wagon in Hallie's eyes.

I still wasn't making many friends, but I was managing to keep out of everyone's way and vice versa. No one seemed too bothered by me one way or the other. The only difficult times were when I had to go to my locker. The lockers were very small and the girl right next to me was very popular. Making my way through the crowd was always something of a challenge. It was for that reason that

I decided it was best to just carry my things with me. I usually stopped at my locker during lunch since everyone else was at the cafeteria. So far it was working out pretty well.

Gym was still my least favorite hour of the day, but it was also the shortest and the easiest. All I had to do was make sure I brought gym clothes and run. So, no complaints. All the other girls in gym seemed to use the time as gossip hour, especially while changing. It was like CNN for high school. Being in gym was the only reason I knew who was dating whom and who hated whom. I heard about fights, dates, and crushes. Some of the information was way more than I would ever want to know, but I just kept my mouth shut.

Hallie, of course, was the subject of all the current discussions. Being new and gorgeous created quite the stir. All the girls wanted to be her friend because all the boys seemed to be within a very short radius of wherever Hallie was.

A couple of girls had tried to get to know Hallie through me. As soon as it became clear that I wasn't going to help with that effort, I was left alone.

I hated to admit it, but I was lonely. In Chicago, even though I was by myself, I still felt like I was part of a group. My group was just one that preferred things quiet. I didn't know their names, but we all sat by ourselves, yet somehow together, in the courtyard behind the school. There was the illusion that I was with other people. In Wabash there was no illusion, I was simply alone.

I heard my name come up in the locker room before gym. The words "snob" and "stuck up" were being used to describe me. I heard someone suggest that I try to be more like my sister. It wasn't uncommon for my severe shyness to be misdiagnosed as snobby and stuck up. I tried not to let it bother me.

* * * * * * * * * * * * * * * *

I woke up in the middle of the night. I was shaking. The dream I had… it was terrifying. I usually wasn't one to dream, but that dream was real.

I dreamed that I was warm, the kind of warm that I would feel when laying on the beach with the sun soaking into my skin. Initially the sun was shining and everything was green and beautiful. I knew I was lost, but it didn't seem to bother me because the beauty that surrounded me was so comforting.

The sun was still shining, but snow began to fall. I wasn't cold even though the snow was covering me.

Without warning everything around me started to die. Everything was turning black; the sky, the trees, the ground. It was so dark... The snow falling was no longer white. It was red, a deep red, almost black. As it landed it turned into blood. I tried to run, but I couldn't move. Something, someone, was coming at me. I couldn't see a face. It was just a black being. I tried to scream but couldn't. The darkness was getting closer.

That's when I woke up. Even though I was awake I felt myself struggling for air. That was the first time the nightmare found me.

* * * * * * * * * * * * * * * * *

It was raining. Mr. Roberts didn't seem to care. We were still going outside to the track.

"The 500 meter dash... it is a sprint. Run until you feel like you are losing control. Run until you are physically unable to stop." True to his word gym class had become an unofficial track practice. Most of the kids grunted and groaned about having to run. I was sort of looking forward to it. I wasn't much for distances, but I loved going fast.

"Line up in groups of three. You will race against whoever is in your line." Everyone was trying to go in the last group. It didn't matter to me whether I went first or last. I walked right up to the line. Immediately after I got in place two guys stood next to me, one on each side, with smirks on their faces; as if it would be a proud moment for them to beat me.

"Ready… Set… Run!" I was off. I didn't care if I was last or first. I just ran. I could feel the heat forming between my feet and the pavement. I could feel the wind on my face. The rain stung as it hit my skin. I just ran. I didn't pay any attention to the runners on either side of me. I didn't want to break my concentration. I kept running even after I crossed the finish line. I didn't want to slow my pace down until I was certain I had gone over the line.

Mr. Roberts was staring at me. He kept glancing between his stopwatch and my feet as if something wasn't right. I saw the other guys laughing at the two who went against me. I wasn't sure what the joke was.

It took a second to sink in. I had beaten both of them. I had beaten those two, muscular, athletic guys. I felt a smile cross my face. I couldn't help it. It wasn't a world record, but I would remember that moment for a very long time. I had never won anything before. I knew I liked running, but I had never compared myself to anyone. I never knew if I was any good.

My speed a caused a bit if a buzz among those I knew to be track members. I wasn't sure what my time had been, but it must've been decent or I wouldn't have won.

"Next!" was Mr. Robert's reply. I could tell he didn't want to make a big deal about my win, but I couldn't help but see a smirk on his face.

Back in the locker room the conversations were no longer about Hallie. I guessed they were about me as the girls were speaking in whispers.

"You're Sidney, right?" I looked up from tying my shoe.

I just nodded without speaking. She was probably just wanting to meet Hallie.

"That was a pretty impressive race."

"Thanks." I went back to putting on my shoes.

"Um… I'm Kelly. If you ever need anything…" She stood there for awhile before starting to walk away.

"Hey Kelly?" I saw her stop to turn around. "Did I really beat them by a lot?"

She shot me a wide smile. "They weren't even close."

"Does that happen? I mean, are they slow?"

"You just beat the best two athletes this school has," she laughed as she walked away toward her locker.

The smile came automatically. I felt... proud. It was a nice feeling to have.

After my big victory I started getting attention from the track team members. They were generally a losing team and really wanted someone to help them win some points. I had no interest in running track. Running was something I did just for me. Besides, I generally wasn't the competitive type.

* * * * * * * * * * * * * * * *

It had been a particularly long day at school, I just wasn't ready to go home. I had no interest in listening to Hallie talk about her perfect day nor did I have any interest in listening to either of my parents give me advice on how to make friends. I had my gym clothes with me... I decided to go for a run.

Going running for me wasn't about completing a set distance. It was about going fast. I loved pushing myself to the limit. I loved the feeling of the wind on my face; the sensation that I was flying. It was the only thing I could do that made me feel powerful.

I drove out of the city limits and parked my car along the side of the road. I got out of the car and just started running. I ran until my legs were on fire. I ran until the oxygen in my body had been depleted. I ran until I was certain that I would trip over my own feet if I continued. I had no idea how far I went or for how long I had been gone. I had no agenda.

I ended up at a crossroads right outside of town. I looked around to examine my surroundings. I had never been there before. I quickly noticed a herd of runners coming right at me. I recognized several members of the pack from gym. I wanted to turn around and, literally, run away. However, my gut told me to stay in order to help my effort of trying to fit in. Plus, I generally liked most of them and wouldn't mind saying hello.

"What are you doing out here?" I was surprised that Kelly stopped to talk. "Out for a run?"

"Sort of... just for fun."

"You should run with us! We are getting ready for the spring track season. We are always looking for new people..." She was a natural recruiter.

"Thanks but I'm not really into track."

"Well, you should at least think about it. There aren't tryouts or anything. Anyone the wants to run is welcome to. Mr. Roberts just puts people where he thinks they fit best. And a lot of colleges are looking for track runners. There are rumors of a few scholarships this year. You never know..."

"Yeah, I will think about it... Well, I had better get going, you know, before it gets too dark."

"Sure thing... I had better go catch up with my group. See you tomorrow!" She waved and then ran off.

* * * * * * * * * * * * * * * *

When I got home everyone else was eating dinner. I didn't realize that a family mealtime had been scheduled.

"Sorry... I didn't know you were cooking." Mom looked irritated. I knew that when she cooked she wanted everyone present and she wanted everyone to savor and enjoy the prepared meal slowly verses the usual inhalation of food that we all were accustomed to.

"I tried to call you... you left your cell in your room. Where have you been?" Mom was the only one speaking. Dad didn't dare speak when Mom was this angry. Hallie was covering up her face with her napkin. She didn't want Mom to see her laughing.

"I was out running." Upon hearing this Hallie snorted causing food to shoot out of her nose. I wished I had that on camera…

"You run?" Dad was immediately interested.

"Yes, I do." Hallie's expression in response to my answer was infuriating. She was trying to control her laughter causing her entire face to turn red. I was sure that she was picturing me as an elephant barreling down the road. "In fact, I am going out for track." I couldn't help but say it. I wanted the laughter to stop. I deserved more respect than that. It was amazing to me that I had been running pretty much all my life and until now no one seemed to notice.

"Sidney that's wonderful!" My surprise announcement seemed to change Mom's mood in the right direction. It looked like I was getting out of missing family dinner.

"Yeah, I was talking to this girl, Kelly, and she was telling me about potential scholarships and stuff…"

"It will take a lot of hard work and dedication to get that kind of attention. We need to make a schedule and get you the right kind of training…." Why did Dad always have to blow everything so way up out of proportion?

"No Dad... it isn't like that. I really do just like running. I don't want to ruin it. It is more for fun than anything else. Besides, they might not let me run. I may not be fast enough."

"That's why you need to practice." As if Dad ever ran a day in his life. He was an average size, I guess, but exercise was not part of his daily routine. It was very typical for Dad to give advice on a subject he knew nothing about.

"That's what after school practice is for. So, sorry Mom... It looks like I won't be getting home until early evening. No family dinners for me...." I didn't even know what the schedule was. Still, if it got me out of family time, then I will take it.

* * * * * * * * * * * * * * * *

During gym I became the person no one wanted to run against because I beat everyone. No one liked losing, especially to me.

After my big announcement at dinner I knew I had to talk to Mr. Roberts about joining track. I still didn't particularly want to join, but anything was better than having to endure family time at home.

Mr. Roberts was the only person who pretended not to care about my running ability. I was getting the impression that he really wasn't interested in having me as part of the team.

"Mr. Roberts?" I spoke so softly that I wasn't even sure if he heard me.

"What's up?" He barely looked up from his clipboard.

"I was wondering about track… are you still looking for runners?"

"We generally don't have tryouts… our unofficial practices are four days a week after school. Practices consist of long distances and sprints. Regular season starts in the spring. Can you commit to that?"

"Sure thing…"

"See you on Monday." With that he walked away.

Great, so that job was done. I was now officially a member of the track team.

OCTOBER

Life had changed with the introduction of track. I still kept to myself, but it was comforting to have familiar faces at school. It was nice being a part of something, even if it was just track. The hours after school were no longer spent alone at the beach. Instead I was running. By the time I got home I was exhausted. Dinner was usually over which meant I was allowed to go directly upstairs.

Homecoming was approaching. It wasn't hard to notice since that was the only thing anyone cared to talk about. Hallie had, without surprise, ended up on the junior class Homecoming court. She was dating one of the football players, which I was certain didn't hurt her cause.

I woke up early the Saturday before Homecoming despite the fact that my alarm didn't go off. That didn't bother me too much as I was an early morning person anyway. I laid in bed for awhile just enjoying the fact that I didn't have to get up. After a few minutes I rolled out and started to get ready for the day. After washing my face and brushing my teeth I decided that my usual jeans and sweatshirt would suffice as my outfit for the day. It wasn't like I was going to prom or anything. My only plan was to go to my beach and hang out. The weatherman forecasted nice weather for the weekend. I didn't know how much longer the fall weather would last, so I wanted to take advantage of it whenever I could.

I went downstairs to grab some breakfast before leaving.

"Morning Sidney!" Mom was still there. I thought she had to leave for work earlier than this. It was almost 8am.

"Not working today?"

"I don't have to be there until ten. The pharmacy opens later on the weekends." My mother the pharmacist... She hated her job so far. The hours were almost as annoying as her co-workers, but she coped well. At least she was like me in the "suffer in silence" way. After a bad day at work, Mom preferred to simply go to her room and shut the door. She was good about not taking it out on the family.

"So you get home late then, huh?"

"I won't be home until well after dinner. Is Hallie up yet? I thought I would make waffles, they are her favorite." So, Mom was going out of her way to make Hallie's favorite? I wouldn't take it personally.

"Not even close. I heard her on the phone until pretty late last night. I doubt she makes it downstairs much before breakfast."

"You talking about me?" Sometimes it seemed Hallie's only purpose in life was to prove me wrong.

"Why are you up? I figured you would sleep for awhile longer."

"We are decorating the school for Homecoming. Everyone will be there today," she gave me a sideways glance, "at least everyone that matters."

"You want waffles Hallie? I am happy to make them." I loved and respected my mother, but sometimes her attempt at being Donna Reed was overwhelming.

"Not today. I have to get going. We have to make posters and put up streamers… there is a lot involved in getting the school ready for the big week." As the words came out of her mouth a car pulled up into the driveway and started honking the horn. "There's my ride!" And she was gone.

"Sorry about the waffles. I am sure they would have been super." Mom looked disappointed, but that was Hallie for you. Never able to appreciate what was being given to her, even if it was just waffles. "Where's Dad?" It was unusual for him not to be up by now.

"He left awhile ago to go to work on his office. He mentioned something about wallpaper and crown molding. I imagine that he will be there for most of the day." Just as I had hoped, everyone would be busy so no one would notice me or my absence. Not that I had anything devious in mind, I just didn't feel like sharing, that's all.

"Don't you want to go with your sister and help decorate the school? It sounds like fun and I am sure that a lot of people will be there, it wouldn't be like you would have to be with Hallie all day."

"Not really my thing Mom. No worries." I ran back upstairs and went to my room to hang out for awhile. I didn't really want to leave until after Mom left for work. I didn't want her to wonder where I was running off to.

I heard her car pull out of the garage after about an hour or so. I grabbed my iPod, my journal, a pen, and my copy of 1984. I had to read it for a project for English class. Once I had everything in my bag, I went out to the wagon and drove off. I was still driving in silence as I had yet to make a CD and the radio stations hadn't changed. I didn't mind the quiet though.

When I arrived at the beach I grabbed my bag and stepped out of the car. I headed to a fallen tree that I had discovered a couple of weeks ago. It was big enough for me to sit comfortably on and it offered a great view of the water. I needed to write in my journal first, to get it out of the way. I had my dream again the night before. I wanted to get it on paper to see if any of it made sense. Writing it down didn't seem to help. Thinking about it still gave me chills.

Once I finished I, again, tore out all the pages and ripped them into tiny pieces. I found the nearest trashcan to dispose of the shreds. While walking to the trashcan I noticed a path that I had not seen before. I was feeling adventurous so I decided to see where the trail would take me.

It didn't appear to be a heavily used path. It wasn't extremely obvious that the pat even existed. I had to pay close attention to where I was walking so that I wouldn't end up on my face.

It was hard not to notice how beautiful everything looked. The sun bounced off of the colorful leaves in the same fashion that it did the water. The reds, yellows, and oranges of fall seemed to be magnified here. It was like walking through a different world. There was nothing like this in Chicago, at least not that I had found.

I walked for what seemed to be a mile or so. I looked to my left and saw a branch of the trail that went closer to the water. It didn't take long for me to end up at one end of an old dock. It stretched all the way to middle of the reservoir. I began to walk down the dock. I couldn't help myself; I was drawn to the water.

I was about halfway to the middle when time seemed to stop. I was cold. I couldn't breathe. I didn't really understand what was happening. Water was rushing all around me. I must have stepped on a rotten board and fallen through; although, I didn't remember falling. I had to swim to the surface. I didn't realize how deep the water was. I was a good swimmer. This shouldn't have been a huge problem. Something kept pulling me down. I couldn't get to the top. I must have been caught in weeds or something. My lungs started to burn. Don't panic. I have always heard that: don't panic. I tried to swim down to free my legs from whatever I was caught on. I had to breathe. The harder I tried to get free the more tangled I became. I kicked and yanked but nothing seemed to work. My throat was on fire. My whole body began to ache. Air. I needed air.

Desperate thoughts began filling my head. No one knew I was here. No one would know where to find me. I was all alone…

Somehow I was able to move my legs again. Something, someone, was pulling me up. I felt my face break through the surface of the water. Air. I didn't open my eyes. I didn't try to speak. Breathe. That was all I wanted to do.

Someone was forcing me out of the water into what seemed to be a very small, unstable boat. I wasn't much help as my whole body still ached from the struggle. I was desperately holding onto someone. I didn't know who it was. I was afraid to let go. I was afraid of going under again.

I tried to talk but my chest and throat still burned. I forced my eyes to open. There was the proof, I was dead. If not that, then I was suffering from severe brain damage. He had to be some sort of angel; although, I had always imagined angels wearing all white and having wings. He was in jeans and a sweatshirt. The sun was directly behind his head creating a halo of sorts. He was beautiful.

Upon willing myself to sit up, reality hit. I became immediately aware that I wasn't, in fact, dead and that he was, in fact, very real. I had not seen him at school. I would have remembered his face. It was the face that sculptors must have used to create masterpieces. His jaw line formed a square around the bottom of his face. His lips were…. Shivering!

I had yet to realize how cold I was. We were both soaked to the core. His shaggy brown hair was causing a steady flow of water to run down his face. I hated to think about what I looked like.

"You okay?" His voice melted me. It was the most beautiful sound I'd ever heard. "You're bleeding…" He pointed to my face.

"I think so…. Thanks." I touched my cheek. I could feel it now. The wood must've scratched my skin as I fell through. "It doesn't hurt."

I didn't know what to say. I had lost all of my words. It wasn't just the fact that he was amazing to look at, it was also the fact that he just saved me from drowning.

How was I supposed to thank someone for that kind of heroism?

"I think you are supposed to try and stay awake after… you know. Think you can, stay awake I mean?" As if I could fall asleep while sitting next to him…

"Sure thing… I'm not feeling tired."

"My name is Scott Andrews."

"Sidney… Sidney Mitchell."

"So Sidney Mitchell," he said wearing a grin on his face, "what were you doing out here?"

"Just looking around. My family just moved here so I was trying to… I guess I don't really have a good excuse."

"No judgment. I was just making conversation. You go to school here?"

"I'm a senior at the high school."

"Which one?" There was more than one? The one I went to barely had enough students to call itself a school.

"I go to Wabash. You?"

"I'm a senior over at Northfield. It is a little smaller than Wabash; it is north, just outside of the city limits."

I didn't ask him where he was rowing us to. I just figured that I would walk to my car from wherever we landed. I wouldn't be picky.

As we approached the shore line I saw a large group of people our age. Please don't let this get complicated. In my head I was imagining ambulances, crying parents, a laughing sister. Attention. I really didn't want this going around at school. Please just let this be no big deal.

"There you are! And with company?" Scott's friends ran toward us. I immediately felt surrounded. Here we go... The fact that Scott and I were both totally soaked was not going to make this any easier. The truth was bound to come out sooner rather than later.

"I caught a big one this time!" I was glad to see that Scott was ready to play this down rather than vice versa. "Sidney, this is Emily, Trevor, and Paul."

"Well, it's nice to meet you," Emily gave the impression that she wasn't exactly thrilled about my unexpected arrival. "I wish it could be under better circumstances. Are you sure you're okay?" As the words left Emily's mouth I could feel a blanket being wrapped around me.

"Really, I'm fine. Scott got to me just in time. This isn't a big deal." The guys were starting to resume their activities from before our arrival. I took that as a good sign.

I looked over my shoulder just in time to see Scott take his shirt off to replace it with another, drier, one. It was hard not to stare. Every muscle in his body was perfectly defined. There was no part of him that I didn't want to look at. While shirtless he shook his head causing extra water from his hair to fly everywhere. I was afraid that I would have to wipe the drool off of my face. He shot me a smile. Even his teeth were perfect; all straight and white. I didn't know guys like him actually existed. I just figured that there was a human zoo somewhere where all the beautiful people were kept until needed for some soap or Diet Coke commercial.

"He's hot, right?" Emily must have seen my jaw drop open. Although, it wasn't like I was hiding it.

"Well, he's not ugly."

"He doesn't date, sorry. I have known him all my life. He had a girlfriend once, but that ended badly and very suddenly. I still don't know what happened with her. He never talks about it and he hasn't dated anyone since." I appreciated Emily's willingness to provide information. "I am not saying he wouldn't be into you, but… I would hate for you to get your hopes up."

"No, it wasn't like that. I was just enjoying the view." We both smiled and laughed it off. Never in my life would I ever think that a guy like Scott would be interested in me. Never…

"Hey Sid! Need a ride back to your car?" Was Scott really going to give me another opportunity to be alone with him?

"That would be great." My heart was already pounding.

Scott drove a beat-up black Chevy truck. It looked ancient. The black had faded and was now more of a charcoal color. The seats had gray upholstery with holes created from wear. It was perfect. The inside of the truck smelled intoxicating. I couldn't help but close my eyes and take in a deep breath. I could feel the effect all the way to my toes. I was glad I was sitting because I was certain I would have fallen over if I had been standing up. It was the perfect combination of soap, aftershave, and whatever else Scott used as part of his daily hygiene routine. I hoped that my clothes would absorb some of the smell so that I could remember this moment forever. I wanted to go home and still be able to know what Scott smelled like.

It was a short drive back to my car as the reservoir wasn't that big. I fully expected Scott to simply drop me off and leave without looking back. Instead he got out to walk me to my car.

"Actually, I have to walk back to the dock to get some stuff that I left behind before all the drama started." I hated saying the words because I knew he would leave and I wasn't quite ready to say good-bye. However, I had to go get my stuff.

"Great, I'll walk you there. I wouldn't want you to fall back in."

"Thanks, but you don't have to." I already felt guilty enough having imposed so much on what was supposed to be his last great day at the beach.

"I feel personally responsible for you. I need to make sure you get home okay. I am still not totally convinced that you are fine." He took my chin in his right hand. My knees buckled. My heart pounded. All I could do was smile. There was no way I was going to attempt to talk.

He dropped his hand and started walking towards the trail. "You coming?"

"Uh, yeah…." I followed quickly after him.

"So, you were out here all by yourself on a perfect day like today? You couldn't con anyone into coming with you?"

"Well… I sort of wanted to just come by myself. I kind of like it quiet." I felt stupid. I shouldn't have said anything. He probably had a million friends who doted on him constantly. Intentionally being alone was most likely not something he would understand.

"I get it… How do you like it here so far? The city school treating you okay?"

"I wouldn't exactly call Wabash a 'city' school. It's pretty country."

"Being country isn't necessarily a bad thing." He shot me that wonderful smile again. I had to remember to breathe…

After a few minutes talking with Scott became effortless. He seemed totally interested in everything I was saying. Nothing about his demeanor implied that I was boring and/or a freak. He was so easy to talk to.

"So, why did your parents move you to Wabash? I mean, I would think that they would rather stay in Chicago than move out to the sticks."

"Some of Hallie's friends were getting into trouble… I think Mom and Dad were afraid Hallie would sort of follow along."

"What kind of trouble?" Scott's interest was surprising.

"Drinking and stuff like that. Nothing terribly criminal… Dad thought that if we moved out here she would be less likely to be influenced."

"I hate to burst his bubble, but stuff like that happens everywhere." Scott looked at me, "They weren't worried about you?"

"I tend to stick pretty much to myself." I didn't want to flat out tell him that I was a dork and that no one wanted anything to do with me. It always sounded better if my loneliness seemed self-inflicted.

"Well, I'm glad they picked Wabash." He winked at me. I felt my heart flutter. I had never had a real crush before. I was amazed at how quickly it had developed.

By the time we got back to the car from retrieving my things the sun was beginning to set.

"Thanks for walking with me. I hope that I didn't ruin your day…" I knew that goodbye was coming.

"Ruin my day? Not possible…." He winked at me. "You think you can make it home okay?" Sure, just as soon as Scott left and I was able to feel my fingers again.

"I think I can manage. Thanks again… for everything. It was great meeting you." I couldn't make myself look him the eyes. I sort of looked over his shoulder so that he wouldn't notice how much he was affecting me.

"I am sure we will meet again soon enough. We play you at Homecoming. You going?" As of yet, I wasn't. I immediately regretted that decision. I had to go. If Scott was going to be there, missing it was not an option.

"I hadn't really given it much thought. It is still a week away. I am not much for planning ahead." I was trying to sound nonchalant, but I felt my voice quivering.

"Well, I'm going…" I couldn't tell if he was asking me to go or not. I didn't want to get my hopes up.

"It's getting dark. I had better get home. My parents don't exactly know where I am." I couldn't believe that I was willingly trying to leave Scott's presence.

"Sure thing. Well… Take care." I watched him walk to his truck. He gave me a final wave and then left.

I sat there for a few minutes. I wasn't yet ready for the day to end. I wanted to go over it again in my head. I wanted to relive Scott touching my face. I wanted to see Scott shirtless again. I was even willing to relive nearly drowning if it meant I could feel myself in Scott's arms just one more time.

Finally, after my heart rate had returned to normal, I left.

* * * * * * * * * * * * * * * * *

It was so dark outside. Surely my alarm clock was lying to me. It couldn't possibly be 7am. It seemed like Wabash was dark all the time. Thank you for that daylight savings time. I managed to make my way to the bathroom without stubbing my toes on any of my still unpacked boxes.

I looked in the mirror. I felt so plain. My eyes looked tired. They were puffy with dark circles. The nightmares weren't doing much for my beauty rest. There had to be something I could do. I closed and locked the bathroom door; I didn't want Hallie to see me going through her things. I opened her drawer and began rummaging. I didn't even know what I was looking for. Which one of her treasures would make me look, well, like her? Since I wasn't in a plastic surgeon's office, I decided to settle on mascara and lip gloss. I left my hair down verses my normal ponytail. I did opt to wear a hair band around my wrist as I knew my hair would eventually get in my face and irritate me enough to be pulled back. Jeans were still my pants of choice. I didn't feel like busting out formal wear. However I chose to wear my lucky t-shirt rather than a sweatshirt. I had found it at a garage sale. It was a vintage Chicago Bears t-shirt with a cartoon of Jim McMahon on the front. It would never be considered high fashion, but I loved it.

Hair down, make-up on, lucky t-shirt... the difference was still only slightly noticeable. I hadn't gone through a major make-over, just enough of one to make me feel one notch higher on the pretty scale. I hoped it wasn't so noticeable that it would draw unwanted attention. It was so stupid. I felt ridiculous. Scott didn't even go to school with me. He wouldn't be there. Why was I trying to impress someone I wasn't going to see? Someone who apparently didn't date anyway.

No one was around when I went downstairs for breakfast. I was certain that Hallie went to school early to finish up any decorating left for the Homecoming festivities. It was a relief to not have to explain my sudden desire to change, somewhat, my outward appearance.

Although I felt as if I looked drastically different, it must not have been noticeable because no one gave me a second glance. Everyone was in a stupor from admiring all the streamers, balloons, and posters which probably took away any attention that might have been directed at me. I really didn't mind.

The school colors were orange and black. To me the decorations made the school look like it was ready for a Halloween party, not a big football game. Hallie looked very proud of her work along with the rest of the decorating committee. All the black streamers made the ceiling look as if it had thrown-up licorice. The girls in their black outfits with orange glitter looked like they were headed to some sort of gothic funeral.

I noticed posters on the wall advertising tickets to the football game and dance. Now, after meeting Scott, there was no question as to my attendance, I had to be there.

I made my way through the crowd to my locker only to notice, with horror, that my locker had been decorated with tiny black pom poms. Black glitter outlined the shape of my locker while orange glitter covered the entire central portion. I tried to look indifferent about the new décor rather than repulsed. As I put my bag away and gathered the required supplies for the day I noticed that my entire body seemed to sparkle. The glitter was rubbing off onto everything. Awesome. At least everyone seemed to be coated in it; not just me.

The rest of the week was more of the same. The buzz was still about Homecoming. Everyone was looking forward to the big game. If a streamer fell, Hallie was there to attach another one. She carried glitter with her in case she saw any bare spots. Nothing was going to spoil this for her. She was, of course, looking forward to being paraded around the football field by her super quarterback boyfriend as part of the Homecoming Court. I was still just trying to figure out how to get to the game. I could go, of course. I just really didn't want to go alone.

After school Mr. Roberts had us a do a distance run. I wasn't thrilled. Under normal circumstances I would've pushed through the run as quickly as possible to get it over with. Today, however, I had an agenda. I needed to get invited to Homecoming.

I ran at a slower pace in order to stay with the pack.

"You going to run with us today?" Kelly laughed.

"Yeah… actually I have been meaning to talk to you." I couldn't believe how nervous I was. "Are you going to homecoming?"

"Sure, who isn't? Why? You want to come with?"
I was so glad that Kelly did all the work for me.

"That would be awesome."

"No problem." Kelly was getting winded. I had
unintentionally picked up the pace. "We can talk details
later, okay?"

"Great." I couldn't help but smile. I was going to
Homecoming!

* * * * * * * * * * * * * * * *

Friday finally came. The clock couldn't move fast
enough. I just wanted the school day to be over. Kelly
informed me that she would pick me up around 6pm for
the game. The game didn't start until 8, but we were going
to tailgate before hand.

I spent the entire day worrying about what I was
going to wear and how I would do my hair. I knew when it
came down to it I would wear jeans and a t-shirt, but I still
toyed with the idea of mixing it up. Hallie had picked out
her fashion statement for the evening days ago. She had
laid out on her bed black tights with a black sweater dress.
She was going to put orange markings on her face to
express her school spirit. I was not. I knew she would

freeze in her outfit of choice, but I kept my mouth shut. My opinions were definitely not welcomed.

I had yet to tell anyone in my family that I was going to the game. I didn't want to listen to the pep talks all week. I was lucky in the fact I knew Hallie wouldn't be home at all after school. She and her new friends were all getting ready together at someone else's house. Dad's car wasn't in the garage. Hopefully I would be able to escape with just leaving a note.

"Sidney? That you?" Mom was home.

"Yeah... it's me." I walked in the kitchen where she was throwing what looked to be quite a variety of items into the crock-pot. I threw my bag on the counter. "What're you making?"

"Well, I figured that with Hallie gone tonight and your dad working late, everyone can just help themselves to this stew or whatever else you can find. Deal?" Even if I was planning on staying home, eating what she was referring to as stew would not have gone on my agenda.

"Sure.. But, Mom? I'm sort of going to the game tonight." She immediately looked right at me, clearly shocked. "I'm going with some people who are going to be on the track team. I guess I should have asked first. Is it okay?" I knew she would say yes.

"That's great! Is someone coming to pick you up? A boy maybe?" I wished it was Scott picking me up.

"No, this girl, Kelly, is going to get me around 6ish."

"That's okay too." Mom was still wearing a smirk on her face that suggested she knew that this might be something more than a friendly gathering. I began to blush, I hoped she didn't notice. I quickly ran upstairs to get ready.

* * * * * * * * * * * * * * * *

Kelly picked me up right on time. I brought with me the mustard and cups that I was asked to contribute as it was a pitch-in of sorts. I felt perfectly comfortable in the jeans and layered t-shirt that I had decided on. I even allowed for lip gloss and mascara knowing that there was a chance Scott would be there. I couldn't help but remember how I looked the last time he saw me.

When we arrived the site was pretty much all set up. Everyone seemed to be already enjoying the hotdogs. I scanned the crowd and tried to hide my disappointment as I didn't see Scott. I had to remind myself that he and I didn't have a date. He had just alluded to the fact that we would both be in the same place at the same time.

"Dig in!" Kelly handed me a hotdog. It actually really did sound good. I hadn't had one in... I couldn't even remember. "I wasn't sure what you liked on yours. I just added some mustard and ketchup; hope that's okay."

"It's better than okay!" I took a ridiculously large bite to try and show my enthusiasm. Kelly glanced over my shoulder and immediately started laughing. I soon learned that the laughter had nothing to do with me or my bite.

"You trying to stay alive today? Or, should I hang around just in case you need the Heimlich?" I was beginning to learn that Scott had impeccable timing.

I tried to respond, but my mouth was still full of hotdog.

"By all means, finish chewing! I saw that bite..." He was still as perfect as I remembered him. He was only wearing jeans and a sweatshirt, but with him wearing the outfit the clothes looked like they were straight from the runway.

"I didn't see you!" I had managed to swallow enough of the hotdog to get out a few words.

"We just got here. I saw you and your friends as we pulled into the parking lot." He was still laughing at me. It was taking an eternally long time for me to get the food in my mouth under control. I had tried to so hard to look perfect and now, again, he was seeing me as a mess.

"Where are you guys setting up?" I asked as I managed to swallow the last of the hotdog.

"We didn't bring a spread like this. We just came a little early to say hi to everyone." He had put his arm around my shoulder, but it was a friendly gesture; not one inspired by feelings that I was hoping he would have.

"Please, help yourself… I am sure we have plenty." I didn't want him to go. I wanted him next to me. Even if he had no interest, his presence was the only thing that I had liked since moving to Wabash.

"That's okay… we're going to see who else is here. I am sure I will see you again before the game is over." He winked and walked back over to his group of friends. I watched as they all just disappeared into the crowd.

I immediately wanted to go home. I no longer had the energy to put on a show. I didn't want to talk to anyone or laugh at their stupid jokes.

"Who was that?" Kelly had gotten over her shock of seeing Scott.

"That was just some guy I met last weekend. We were both over at the reservoir. He was there with some buddies."

"He's gorgeous! Is he dating anyone? Because if he is single… you mind making an introduction?" Even though I could tell Kelly was joking, I still had to wipe the drool from her mouth.

"I really don't know anything about him. All I know is that he is a senior over at Northfield. His last name is Andrews…." I thought maybe she might have heard of him. Everyone around here knew everybody. In a town the size of Wabash, there were no secrets.

"I wonder if he is Max Andrews' kid. That guy is crazy…. His wife died a long time ago and he started drinking… heavily. I know he has kids, but I'm not sure how old they are…." That was some powerful information. Thank you, Kelly.

So, Scott's mom was dead and his dad was a raging alcoholic. But Scott seemed so… normal. Weren't kids from that sort of environment supposed to be all dark and twisted? It didn't matter. It was none of my business and it appeared as if my relationship with Scott was going to be very short lived.

The game was horrible. Wabash lost by an embarrassing amount of points. I hadn't known, but Wabash always lost. From what I heard during the game it didn't matter the sport, Wabash always lost. I had heard they were good a few years back which provided the town with some hope, but once those seniors graduated... well, Wabash always lost.

Kelly and I started the walk back to her car. Our tailgating site along with all the other essentials required for going to a football game had been cleaned up and put away. The night was over, it was time to go home. I heard footsteps behind us, which wasn't unusual since there was a crowd of people heading out to the parking lot. As the steps became louder it was clear that someone was running at me from behind.

"Sidney! Wait up!" I spun around to see who it was yelling at me. Scott almost toppled over me when he tried to stop quickly on the gravel. He bent over and held up one finger telling to me hold on while he tried to catch his breath. Seriously, he didn't run that far. He shouldn't have been that winded.

Kelly shot me a wink, "Sid, I'll just wait for you at the car." I appreciated her understanding.

"Some game huh?" I didn't really want to talk football with Scott. If this wasn't going to amount to anything, I would really rather just go home. "A bunch of us are going to a bonfire up by the lake. You in?" Scott could barely get the words out as he was still winded from his short sprint across the field.

It took me a second to process what he was asking me. What would it hurt to go? My mind and my heart were having a battle. I knew that he didn't want to date me. But yet, why then was he asking me to the bonfire?

"I rode here with Kelly. I don't have a way to get there. Sorry… but thanks for asking." I started to walk towards Kelly's car.

"Hey, if you want to go, I'll give you a ride! That isn't a problem."

"Didn't you ride here with your friends?" I wasn't trying to get out of going, I just needed more information. I didn't want to be stuck in a car full of people that I didn't know.

"We came in three cars. I will have them pile into two of the three. Really, not a problem. So, you interested?" Absolutely. Of course I was interested. I was just scared. I didn't want this to end up being too painful for me. I foresaw heartache in mass quantities in my future if I went.

"Um... sure. That'd be great. I have to go tell Kelly. She is waiting for me at her car, remember?"

"Let's go..." He walked me over to tell Kelly goodbye and then we were off.

Once again I found myself in his truck, a truck that made my wagon look new. There was that smell again. It was going to be impossible for me to contribute coherently to any conversation until the immediate shock of his overwhelmingly powerful aroma wore off. That smell in a bottle would make millions.

Scott slid into the driver's seat. "You don't ride in trucks much, do you?" I felt like he was laughing at me.

"Enough, I guess..." I had been in a truck before. What could I have possibly been doing wrong?

"Not with a guy you haven't... not out here, anyway. You have to sit in the middle so that I can get my arm around you. I can't reach you all the way over there." He was smiling his brilliant smile. He knew. He had no doubt that all I wanted was to be close to him. His confidence shook me. Without saying a word I looked at him and scooted myself over toward the middle seat.

The middle seat was not comfortable. I had to rearrange my legs in an awkward way in order to fit. I was sitting on something incredibly hard. I had to wiggle around until I found a section to, sort of, land myself in. All of that faded away as soon as I felt his warmth on my arm. I wanted to put my head on his shoulder. I wanted to snuggle my face into the crook of his neck. His arm reached around me and pulled me closer to him.

"What is it about you?" It was hard to see what his face was saying as he was driving and it was dark.

"I don't know what you mean..." I really didn't.

"I met you less than a week ago and here we are. I can't wait to get you to the bonfire and show you off." I could see the side of his face curve up. I still didn't know what was going on, but I wasn't about to fight over it. I was going to enjoy this ride for as long as I possibly could.

"Here we are? Where is that exactly?" I was anticipating some sort of sarcastic answer to my question; perhaps the name of the street we were currently on.

"I don't know... you sure are a lot different from the girls around here. Most of the girls wear ribbons in their ponytails and are afraid to eat in front of people. Either that or they are dying their hair black and wearing black nail polish to make a statement about conformity. When I saw you stuff half that hotdog in your mouth... I almost lost it." I wanted to shrink down into the floorboard. I was humiliated. I didn't want to be his comic relief.

"Kelly really wanted to meet you. She thinks you are... well, you know."

"And what do you think? That's the more important question." I wondered how much longer we had to drive until we got to the fire. I was sorry I brought this up. I didn't want to talk to him about my feelings.

"Well, I am sure you know that you are... I mean it is pretty obvious." He pulled into the parking lot as the words left my mouth. He grabbed a baseball cap and put it on. He handed me a cowboy hat.

"What is this?" I held it like it was going to bite me or something. Was I expected to wear that?

"Trust me, you will feel a lot more comfortable wearing that than not. Remember, you're in the country now." Reluctantly I put the hat on. "Wow... that look really suits you." He took my hand and we walked toward the crowd.

I was glad to see that I recognized some faces. Trevor was helping build the fire. He waved and motioned for Scott to join him.

"It's fine, go. I would like to say hi to Emily anyway."

"Cool... just come find me, okay?" His goofy grin returned and he ran over to help his friends.

I found Emily sitting with some other people on the giant logs that formed a circle around the flames. When she saw me she waved and motioned for me to come over.

"Hey there! Glad you could make it... Did Scott bring you?" Emily didn't seem to mind that I was there. But I am sure that my escort was confusing her as his reputation for dating didn't seem to match his current actions.

"It was sort of a last minute thing. He found me after the game. It's not a big deal, really." I was dying to ask her if the rumors I had heard about his family were true. I didn't know how to bring it up, or if it was even appropriate. I decided to just let it go for the time being. I didn't want anything to spoil the night.

"I don't mean to butt in your business, but like I said the other day... Just be careful when it comes to attaching yourself to Scott. He is a great friend, and I love him for that, but... " She just shook her head as if that would finish the statement for her.

"But...?" I needed more information.

"He just doesn't date. I don't want him to give you the wrong impression." I wondered if Emily was just jealous because she cared for Scott more than she let on. I hated to think that, but so far Scott had done nothing to make me think he was anything other than a really good guy.

"Thanks for the warning. But like I said, this really isn't anything..." I didn't want Emily to know how I really felt. Especially if she wanted more from Scott than what he was giving her.

I had to admit that the bonfire was awesome. Someone had brought speakers and placed them in the back of a truck. Although the music was country, I still liked it. There was something about being there... no one cared what anyone looked like. (That was obvious because everyone was wearing flannel shirts and hats). Everyone was laughing and just having a good time.

Scott roasted marshmallows for me. He insisted that the only way to do it right was to catch the marshmallow on fire. That way a nice black sugar crust would form on the outside. I didn't know I was supposed to put the whole thing in my mouth at once. I bit into it and instantly marshmallow goo oozed down my face and all over my clothes. Again, I was making a mess.

"You are great, you know that, right?" Scott took his sleeve and wiped my face clean, sort of.

"This is not me being great... I promise." What was so awesome about me being covered in hot, sticky marshmallow?

Before I could get a chance to think of something really clever to say, I unexpectedly felt his mouth on mine. I had never been kissed before. I had never dated before. I didn't know what to do. I just froze. It was so... sudden.

He backed away. "I'm sorry... I thought..."

"Scott... not here, okay? Somewhere... less...populated? Maybe?" I didn't want to tell him that he was my first kiss in front of all of his friends. Most girls had kissed a guy by high school. Hallie got her first kiss when she was in eighth grade. I didn't want him to think that there was something wrong with me.

He took my sticky hand and led me back toward the truck. We didn't get in, we just stood outside.

"Sid… I'm really sorry. I didn't mean to offend you or…"

I quickly interrupted him, "No, it wasn't that. It's just that I am covered in goo and I am certain that I look the part. I just didn't think you thought of me that way. I wasn't sure… I didn't want my first kiss to be… " I felt so stupid. Tears were welling up in my eyes. In my head I could hear his laughter. I could see him running back down to the beach and telling all of his friends. I was preparing myself for the long walk home as I was sure he no longer had any interest in letting me ride in his truck, especially in the middle seat.

"That was your first kiss?" The sincerity in his voice surprised me. I nodded my head. "You are right, then. That's not the way it should have happened. I can do better than that," he smiled.

He pulled me close to him. I could feel the heat from his body. He was so warm. He smelled like burning leaves and aftershave. He placed his hands gently on my face. He bent down as if to kiss me. I waited for it. He was inches away from my face.

"We will do this the right way," he whispered. "Can I see you tomorrow?" He wasn't going to kiss me... I could have fainted. The anticipation was killing me. I thought for sure...

"Tomorrow would be great." I was amazed that I was still able to speak.

He gave me a squeeze and motioned for me to get in the truck.

"You live in the old Thomas house, right?"

"Yeah.. How did you know?" I had never referred to my house as that.

"Small town, no secrets. Remember?" With that he turned the car on and drove me home.

* * * * * * * * * * * * * * * * * *

I didn't want to open my eyes the next morning. I wanted to replay the movie in my mind from the night before. Did Scott really kiss me? It had to have been a dream. Moments like that didn't happen in real life yet somehow I could still feel his hands on my face. Excitement began to grow within me as I remembered our plans for the day.

I forced myself to look at the clock. It was only 6am. Scott wouldn't pick me up until noon. I had no idea what we were doing or where he was taking me. His only instructions were to be ready on time and to wear warm clothes. Six hours seemed an eternal amount of time to wait. How was I going to occupy myself?

I threw on my gym clothes, grabbed my tennis shoes, and bolted downstairs. I knew that going for a run would kill about an hour or so, depending on how long I felt like going once I got started.

"You didn't get in until pretty late… Hallie beat you home." I jumped. I hadn't expected to see anyone as it was still so early. Dad was waiting for an explanation. I knew that I was going to have to tell him something, but I just wasn't ready to divulge anything about Scott. I didn't want to hear a lecture about how high school kids shouldn't have boyfriends or about dating. I really didn't want to get the sex talk again. For a dad, he really liked bringing up the subject of protection and teenage pregnancies.

"We hung around the field for awhile after the game. Then, we all went to the reservoir for a bonfire. It was pretty cool…" It wasn't really a lie, I just left out a few, minor, details.

"Call next time."

"Sure thing… I always forget my phone, sorry."

"Big plans for today? Hallie's going to the school to tear down the decorations. You helping?"

"No, Dad. I just thought I would go for a run before the rest of the world wakes up. After that, I don't really know…" That was true. I honestly didn't know what my plans were. Again, I was just leaving out a few minor details.

"Well… I'm off. Enjoy your day." Dad got up and threw out the remainder of his coffee. "If you see your mother will you tell her I'll be home early?"

"Sure thing Dad."

As soon as I saw Dad's car pull away from the driveway, I was out the door. My legs felt great. There was no stopping me today. I could run forever. I was listening to my usual playlist, but I yearned for the country songs I had heard the night before. In my mind I was still wearing that ugly cowboy hat. I could still feel the heat from the fire on my face. Then, his kiss. No matter how short lived it was, it would last forever in my memory.

While running I fantasized about what it would mean to be Scott Andrews' girlfriend. I knew so little about him. I didn't trust the rumors to be sources of accurate information. Besides, his family history made no difference to me. All that mattered was him.

I thought of Scott. He shouldn't already mean this much to me. Somehow, he had changed my life here. I wanted to... I wanted to look at him. Smell him. I was forced to stop running upon remembering that intoxicating smell. Just thinking about his warmth sent chills throughout my core. I decided to head back home... if I kept thinking about Scott I wouldn't get far as breathing was necessary for running; something I kept forgetting to do whenever his image came into mind.

I was disappointed to see when I got home that it was still several hours before Scott would pick me up. I had to keep myself busy. I went out to the garage. Dad had purchased the paint for my room several days ago. I had picked out a light blue shade that matched my brown furniture. There was no time like the present to get started on that project.

I moved all my furniture into the middle of my room and covered it with old blankets. Then, I started painting. It took a lot longer than I had imagined. I only finished two walls before it was officially time to get ready. I had paint all over me. No worries, it would all come off in the shower.

I got ready very quickly. I couldn't help it, I was just too excited to move slowly. I was careful to wash off all the blue paint from my arms and face. I was pretty sure that I had gotten all of it out of my hair as well. I slipped on my favorite jeans and sweater. I was miraculously able to find a matching pair of gloves. I wasn't sure if I would need them, but Scott had really emphasized the part about dressing warm.

As soon as I was ready I went downstairs to wait by the window. I wanted to spare him the trip to my front door. I knew it would probably make me seem too eager, but I didn't care. All I cared about was seeing Scott.

I only had to wait a few minutes before I saw his truck turn onto my street. He pulled into the driveway.

"Have you been waiting long? I'm not late, am I?" He yelled out his window. There was that smile…

"No, not late. I was just trying to spare you from having to come inside. That's all." I was certain that he could hear the lie. He had to know that the past six hours had felt like ten years.

"Well… let's go! We got lucky today with the weather. There won't be many days like this left before the snow hits." We got into the truck. Again, he motioned for me to scoot to the middle. I slid down into the seat so that the top of my head would rest comfortably on his shoulder. Instead of putting his arm around me, he grabbed my left hand and held it tight. "You ready?"

"I hope so…. Where are you taking me?"

"Can't tell… besides, words can't describe it. You have to see it to really get the whole effect." I didn't care if he was taking me to slaughter pigs… with him, anything would be perfect.

We drove for awhile without saying anything. I forced myself to look out the passenger window only so that I would stop staring at him. Wherever he was taking me was a place I had never been before. Nothing looked familiar. All I could see were empty corn fields.

The further we drove the more narrow the road became. It was clear to me that wherever we were going was not a place that had many visitors.

"You don't mind taking a walk, right? I mean, you were hiking the other day…" His brown eyes melted me. I would have done anything he asked.

"I am game for whatever you have planned." I looked him in the eyes but had to quickly change my focus.

I could feel the heat rising in my face. I was certain that my cheeks were turning a bright shade of pink.

When the pavement of the road turned to gravel, Scott stopped the truck.

"This is as far as the truck will take us." He helped me out since I was sort of stuck in the middle. As he lifted me out he wrapped his arms tightly around my waist and gave me a good squeeze. I put my arms around his neck and squeezed back. I could have stayed like that forever. My face was buried in his neck. I could feel his pulse through his skin.

"You ready?" He whispered in my ear. As his breath hit my ears a chill went down my back. No, I definitely wasn't ready.

"Sure thing…. " We let go of each other and began walking.

It was clear we weren't going down a path. I wasn't sure how Scott knew where he was. I had lost all sense of direction. I knew that if I got lost I would never be able to find my way back to the truck. I guess my only option was to stay as close to Scott as possible. That would not be a problem.

"Where are we?"

"This is my family's farm."

"How long has it been in your family?"

"My grandparents bought it right after they got married. My dad grew up here. Someday, it will be mine." His voice indicated that he wasn't exactly excited about what he felt his future held for him.

I kept my eyes focused on the ground. I didn't want to trip on anything and land face first in the mud. I was going to try very hard to not turn myself into a disaster this time.

"We're here…" He pointed straight ahead. It was the most amazing thing I had ever seen. He was right, he couldn't have told me. Words would not have done justice to what I was looking at.

It was an old train trestle. But, it was so much more than that. The trees had somehow gotten tangled in the tracks forming a canopy of sorts. There were enough leaves still left on the trees to make it seem like everything was made out of gold. The small amount of water that had collected under the trestle had a reflecting effect making the whole scene appear twice as magnificent.

"How did you find this place? Are we still on your farm?" I couldn't even imagine having something like this in my backyard.

"This is just outside of our property line. This was a working track when my grandparents lived here."

"This is amazing...." I was speechless.

He took my hand and led me to a path that went straight to the top of the trestle.

"Is it safe?" I wasn't sure how comfortable I felt walking out onto the tracks.

"You will be fine, promise. I won't let anything happen to you."

We carefully walked to the halfway point. If I thought the view from the bottom was amazing, then the view from the top was twice that.

"You can see everything from up here. Can you see your house?"

"It is back that way somewhere." He seemed very reluctant to show me where he lived.

He ushered me to sit down. Here we were... In this perfect place; with no one around. My hands were becoming sweaty at a frightening pace. My heart rate was increasing. I could feel each heartbeat as they pounded in my chest. I was shocked that he couldn't hear it.

"Sidney… I don't date." That was so not what I thought he was going to say. Although, it's how I imagined he felt. I wondered if he heard my small world crack in half.

"I had heard something like that."

"You heard? From who? Never mind, it doesn't matter. My point is, I don't date. There are a lot of reasons why but I don't care to go into them right now. It's just that…" He turned his face toward the ground. I heard him take a few deep breaths before he spoke again. "For some reason, I can't get you out of my head." He was looking right at me now. I could feel his stare. I couldn't look back. My eyes were starting to burn. I could feel the tears welling up. He was playing hot and cold with me and it hurt.

He asked me to come here with him. He was the one that had kissed me. He was the one making all the advances. I couldn't sort through it in my head. It wasn't making any sense. I kept telling myself from the first time we met that it couldn't last because he was too good for me. Why was he toying with me like this? I just didn't get the joke.

"Look at me… " I couldn't. I didn't want him to see me cry. "No, look at me…" He took my chin in his hands and turned it so I had to face him. No one had seen me cry… not in a very long time. I couldn't believe he was making another first on my list.

"I didn't mean it like that… I am just trying to figure it out, okay? You are so different from all the other girls…" He was doing it again. Forcing me to let him in even though I knew I wasn't what he wanted.

"You don't know me. You don't know that I am different. You have known me for, like, seven days." I had to say it. I had to say something. I couldn't just let him get away with the pain he was causing me. This was supposed to be a perfect day.

"I know that you can run faster than anyone Wabash has ever seen." I looked at him wondering how he knew. "Small town, remember? I know that you aren't afraid of being true to what you believe in. That's why the other girls aren't getting to you. I know that you love hotdogs. I know you love the color blue…"

"How do you know that?" Surely he couldn't read minds.

"I am guessing since you are wearing a swatch on the back of your neck." I reached back in horror only to realize that he was right. I had missed a spot in the shower. Why couldn't I get it right just once? "I know that you have the prettiest green eyes I have ever seen. I know that I am crazy about you…"

"Why don't you date?" If I was going to continue to let him torture me I had to get some answers to my questions.

"Can we save that conversation for another day?"

"Is there going to be another day… I mean, one with both of us intentionally in the same spot?"

"Is there a reason why there wouldn't be?" He was smiling again. Although, I was certain that the smile was more for my benefit than anything else.

"I need something… answers to questions…. You have to help me understand what is going on." I just wanted him to say something that would help put my heart back together again.

"My mom died a long time ago leaving me and my dad all alone. All of my grandparents are long gone. So it's just the two of us. Dad starting drinking. Dad gets real ugly when he drinks. It can make things… complicated." Scott got very quite. It was like his whole body just stopped. Now it was him that couldn't look me in the face. I could tell there was more to the story. I didn't want to push him. He seemed to feel like he had told me too much already. It didn't matter to me. His family history wasn't going to scare me away. Scott was not his dad.

I took his hand in mine and pulled him over to me. I put his face in my hands.

"It's okay. You don't have to say anymore. Let's just..." Before I could say another word his face was, again, within inches of mine. I could feel the warmth of his breath on my lips. He had one hand on each side of my face. I felt my head spinning. My blood rushing. I knew I wouldn't have been able to count to ten if asked to. He brushed the hair away from my face and tucked it behind my ear. I had to close my eyes. The world was spinning so fast that I was afraid I would fall over. I tilted my head down to try and regain control. He forced it back up with his fingers. Then, he kissed me. It wasn't like the night before. This kiss spoke to me. It told me how he felt. It told me that I mattered.

He pushed his hands into my hair and pulled me as close to him as possible. I wrapped my arms around his neck. Not even the Jaws of Life could've separated me from him.

He moved his lips from my mouth and began tracing my jaw line until he was kissing my neck. Now I was addicted. I knew I wouldn't survive without him. I tugged on his shaggy brown hair. He ran his hands up and down my back without ever letting me go. He held onto the back of my shirt as if trying to eliminate any possible distance than could've been between us. I thought my head was going to explode.

I wished that time could've stopped. That we would never have to leave. He eventually slowed down and loosened his grip. Reluctantly, I followed his lead.

"It will be dark soon." I knew he was right; I just didn't want to admit it.

"I don't want to leave." The idea of leaving this place only to go back home was devastating.

"There is always tomorrow."

"Tomorrow is too far away. What if I can't wait that long?" I couldn't believe that I was allowing my guard to fall so completely. I didn't want to become so vulnerable so fast.

He pulled me into to him again. I felt so small against his broad chest. I could hear his heart beating. I could have fallen asleep just listening to the soft rhythm.

"Tomorrow will be here before you know it, I promise. I won't let another day go by where we don't see each other. Trust me, I too will be counting the minutes until I see you again." We separated and began the walk back to the truck. I didn't force conversation. There were no more words to say. Whether or not he dated was no longer an issue. We were together. As long as that didn't change, I didn't care what the label was.

NOVEMBER

Scott and I were living the happily ever after found at the end of every fairytale. He would be waiting for me in the parking lot every day after track practice. From there we would go to the beach, to the trestle, or on a walk through his fields. It didn't matter where we were or what we were doing as long as we were together. Every second spent away from Scott made my heart ache. I felt hollow when he wasn't around. The anticipation of seeing him distracted me from everything else. When around him, he was all I could focus on. Nothing else mattered.

School was getting better as I was making more friends through track. It was sort of becoming a big deal that I was decent at the sprints. Mr. Roberts even let out a smile once or twice upon reading my times. I knew he didn't want to admit it, but I think he was impressed.

"Is it official yet?" Kelly was trying to talk to me while we were on one of our distance practice runs.

"Is what official?" I didn't much care for socializing while running; especially since the long runs weren't really my thing anyway.

"You and that guy from Homecoming… I heard that you two are inseparable."

"Um… I guess so." I really didn't want to go into the details of my relationship with Scott. We had just started dating, if that's what it could be called. I wasn't ready to hand out information just yet.

"So… is it true about his dad?" This is what Kelly really wanted to know, the gossip.

"We haven't really talked about it. I haven't met his dad yet." I gradually started to pick up my pace. I knew that Kelly wouldn't be able to keep up after awhile and would have to back away.

"Be careful when you do. I heard that he is totally nuts, in a mean way."

"Where did you hear that?" I was still continuing to go faster.

"Some kid from Northfield… he was with Scott at the game. I don't know his name." Kelly's breathing was becoming louder. I could tell she was starting to struggle. "You are going really fast…" Her statement asked me to slow down. Instead, I pushed harder. As planned she had to slow down and I was free to run alone.

As I finished my run I wondered about what Kelly had told me. Surely his dad wasn't that bad… But that could explain why Scott was so insistent on never going to his house. I thought he might be ashamed of his home or something, I hadn't thought that he was trying to protect me from his father.

I finished my run in record time thanks to Kelly. Since these weren't counted as actual practices, we were free to leave as soon as we had completed the exercise for the day. I grabbed my bag and was out the door. This was always the best part of my day; seeing Scott.

There he was… in the parking lot. He parked his truck next to my wagon as usual. He reached out his arms to pull me in.

"You may not want to do that today… I'm pretty gross." It only felt fair to give him a warning.

"Come 'ere…" If I smelled bad, he didn't let on. He just held me close, letting me breathe him in.

"I have an idea…"

"Okay, what's up?"

"Why don't we go to your house? I mean, I have been to your farm, but I want to see where you live. It's only fair, you have seen mine…"

"I have a better idea." Of course he did. "You are already pretty dirty, right?" I didn't feel the need to answer that question out loud. I simply nodded my head. "Feel like playing some football?"

"You are aware that I am a girl, right? I mean, I don't know how to play…"

"Your only job will be to run, promise."

"Is someone going to tackle me to the ground?" I was much more of a spectator when it came to team sports. Catching objects midair was not something I was good at nor was I in the mood to be thrown to the ground.

"You will be fine. It'll be fun, trust me."

We drove out to his farm and parked along side one of his fields. I saw a group of people waiting for us. I recognized Emily and Trevor, but all the other faces were new.

"You sure she's ready for this?" Trevor laughed.

"You'll see, she's my new secret weapon." I wasn't sure why Scott was so confident in my ability to play. I had never played football before.

There were two teams, each having four people.

"Sid is going to play running back." I heard Scott tell the rest of our team. I didn't know what that meant, but I didn't want to ask in front of everyone. "Whatever you do, give her the ball!" Scott's instructions made me nervous, I didn't want anything to do with the ball.

I managed to catch Scott before the game officially started.

"I don't know what you want me to do…." I felt stupid for not understanding the game when everyone else seemed to think it was easy. I would've rather have been taking a Calculus test than playing football.

"See those two cars?" Scott pointed directly in front of me. "Those are our goal posts. When you get the ball, just run. Keep running until you reach the middle of those two cars, got it? That is your only job. I will make sure you get there, deal?"

"What if I get pushed down?"

"This is two-hand touch. If someone gets both of their hands on you, stop running. That's the same thing as being tackled. No one is going to push you down." Scott put both his hands on my shoulders. "You okay?" I nodded. "You're going to be great…"

"I can't catch very well either…" I hated to admit to yet another fault.

"I will hand you the ball, no catching required. Just relax and have fun, okay?" Scott smiled and left to get into position.

My whole body was shaking. I wanted so badly to impress him. I tried to remember his instructions: just run to the cars. I could do this.

Scott yelled some numbers and I watched the guy in front of him throw Scott the ball. As promised Scott gave it immediately to me. I started running. I ran as fast as I could. I saw the cars getting closer. I didn't pay any attention to anything going on around me. I didn't feel anyone's hands on me so I just kept going. I didn't stop until I reached the goal.

I turned around and saw Scott laughing hysterically. What had I done? No one else was laughing, they were all just standing there staring at me.

"I told you she was awesome!" I heard Scott yell. He ran over to me. "See how easy that was?"

"Why are they looking at me like that?"

"Because you were so fast that no one even came close to catching you, that's why." He picked me up and spun me around. I had done something right! Finally! "Now, it is their turn to try and get a touchdown. For this part you are just sort of going to hang out in the back... play safety. If the guy, or girl, carrying the ball gets past all of us... well, then go after them. Remember, get both of your hands on them, that's the only way to stop the play. Got it?"

"I think so..." This part sounded more complicated. I felt better though, more confident.

I heard Trevor say, "Go!" then I watched the guy playing center throw Trevor the ball. I just followed the ball with my eyes. I watched as it was passed to Emily. Scott ran straight to her and stopped her before she could get very far. Emily squealed when Scott put his hands on her. I saw her face light up when Scott put his arm around her shoulder while walking her back to her position. I didn't mind that Emily, obviously, liked Scott. What girl wouldn't? He was perfect; there was nothing not to like. Thinking about that made me wonder why he chose me...

I didn't have much time to think before the next play started. It was like watching a rerun. Trevor gave the ball to Emily and she, again, was stopped by Scott. That happened three times. They only had one more chance to make a play before it was our turn again. I hated to admit it, but this part was sort of boring and was taking forever. Plus, it wasn't the greatest time I'd ever had watching some other girl flirting with my... boyfriend? I wasn't sure what to call him...

I should have been paying closer attention. This time Trevor ran. He didn't pass the ball at all. He just took it and went. Scott couldn't get to him, he had been anticipating another pass to Emily. No one else would reach Trevor in time. It was going to be up to me. I started running toward him as he hadn't passed me yet. I was so close, but I knew my arms wouldn't quite reach. I lunged forward allowing both feet to leave the ground. I felt my hands clasp around some part of him. I closed my eyes when I realized I was going to crash into the ground. I wasn't sure which part of Trevor I was taking down with me.

"I thought you were afraid of tackling?" I heard Scott yell from across the field. There was his laughter again. "Two-hand touch, remember?"

I had grabbed Trevor's leg forcing him to crash into the ground with me.

"I'm sorry... are you okay?"

Trevor was looking at me like I was some sort of crazed animal. "Dude, next time she is on my team!"

Emily was glaring at me. Obviously she was used to being the only girl playing. The fact that I was playing well didn't seem to be helping me win her affections.

It was our turn again to try for a touchdown. This was the easy part… just run. Although, as we were getting into position I could tell that this wasn't going to be as simple as the first try. I was no longer a secret. Everyone was preparing themselves to run after me.

"No worries… you are still way faster than any of them, okay?" Scott whispered over his shoulder. I nodded.

Just like the time before Scott handed the ball to me as soon as the play started. I took the ball and went. I saw my target, same as before. I heard footsteps behind me, lots of them. I pushed myself to go faster. I could tell that I was creating a greater distance as the footsteps seemed to disappear. I stopped when I reached our goal line.

Before I had a chance to turn around I felt a force crash into me causing me to slam into the ground.

"Sidney!" Scott ran to my side.

I looked up at him. "I thought I was inside our goal."

"You were…" Scott glared at Emily. She was wiping away grass from her pants indicating that she had also landed on the ground.

"Sorry about that Sid." The look on Emily's face was not one of regret. I had a feeling that she felt pretty good about her actions. There was no doubt that jealousy was a major factor in her intentions.

Scott held out his hand to help me. "You're bleeding…"

"Where?" I examined my arms and head and felt nothing. Then I saw my leg…

Scott looked around on the ground trying to find what had caused the gash on the back of my thigh. "This must've done it." Scott held out an old piece of glass that had been lodged in the ground. It had my skin on one of the sharper edges. "We're going to have to get that cleaned up…"

I would've argued, but the throbbing had started and I could live without playing another round of football.

"Can you make it alright?" Scott's voice held a tone of guilt. I was sure he was remembering his promise that I wouldn't get hurt.

"I think I can somehow manage. Really, it looks a lot worse than it is."

"I have a first aid kit at home…" I could tell that he wasn't looking forward to taking me to his house.

"So today we both get what we want…" I winked at him.

"Scott… seriously? You can't take her to your house." Trevor's words had a force in them that told me he was very serious.

Scott looked in his direction and nodded his head knowingly, "He's not there. He went hunting this morning. Shouldn't be back until tomorrow at the earliest."

"Who are you talking about?" I asked.

"His dad." Emily answered my question without even looking at Scott. She must've also known the secret that Scott refused to share with me.

"Let's go…" Scott took my hand and led me in the direction of his home.

We walked in silence for awhile, but Scott's enthusiasm couldn't be contained for long.

"Seriously, you were awesome! I mean, I knew you would be good, but… wow!" Scott's praise was all I needed to feel better. Knowing that I had done something to make him happy was all I wanted.

"It's not a big deal… I just did what you told me to…." I couldn't help but smile.

"I didn't tell you to take out Trevor… That was the most incredible play I've seen! You should've seen the look on Trevor's face." Scott's total elation made my heart fly. Nothing in my life that I had ever done mattered as much as this. "You never cease to amaze me."

"Amaze you?" My heart longed for him to elaborate.

"You're always so much more than I expect. Like today, I knew you would be great, but you took it to the next level. You aren't afraid of anything." I didn't want to admit to him that I was afraid of everything, especially him. He stopped walking to kiss me. I didn't feel bad anymore about being sweaty. We were both filthy now.

We finally arrived at his front door. The house before me was comparable in size to my parents' three car garage. It looked as if a strong wind could blow it over. The screen door was barely hanging on. I was afraid to touch it; I didn't want to tear it off of the house.

Scott ushered me inside. The main room was dark. The floor was covered with shaggy brown carpet. The single couch was upholstered with a dingy red and yellow plaid material. Most of the material was so worn through that stuffing was starting to come out. There was a small television sitting in the corner on top of a stand that could collapse at any moment. The walls were covered with dark paneled wood. The mood was oppressive.

Scott motioned for me to follow him into his room. His room was directly off of the main living area. It was small and just as dark. His bed was nothing more than a mattress on the floor in the corner. There was a small window in the far wall, but it was barely big enough to let in any light.

"Here," he pointed to his bed, "have a seat."

"I don't want to get blood on anything."

He placed a clean towel over his blankets. "This will be okay."

I carefully sat down trying not to get blood on his mattress. It was difficult with the cut being on the back of my leg.

Scott left me alone while he left to get his first aid kit from the bathroom. I took his brief absence as an opportunity to scan his room. I wasn't looking for anything specific, just something to help me understand Scott a little more.

There were books everywhere. There must've been close to a hundred of them ranging from "How To's" to revered classics such as Jane Eyre and Pride and Prejudice. Leaning on the back wall was a guitar case. Behind it I saw a box full of letters.

"Here we go…" Scott sat right down next to me with his small box of medical supplies.

I was dying to ask Scott about his assortment of possessions. I hesitated knowing how private he kept his family history. I knew he would tell me when he was ready. I decided not to pry.

"This might sting a little… sorry." He was right. I couldn't help but wince as he applied the alcohol to my open wound. "I can't believe Emily… she knows the rules."

"I can. She is clearly into you, can't you tell?" I surprised myself with my own frankness. The words came out before I had a chance to stop them.

"Yeah… we had to have a talk awhile ago."

"Let me guess, you told her that 'you don't date.'" I made quotation marks with my fingers while repeating my least favorite phrase of his.

"Yep, among other things." Scott finished up his medical duties by applying band-aides to my leg. "There, all better."

"Emily is the one that told me that you don't... well, you know. She also said something about a mysterious disappearance of a previous girlfriend." I thought this was the perfect opportunity to have at least one of my questions answered.

"There was a girl once, but I am pretty sure you aren't interested in that story." I knew Scott was trying to change the subject, but I wasn't going to let him. I was too curious.

"Quite the contrary..."

"Okay, well... Her name was Kate. I thought she was what I wanted. She was the kind of girl I thought I was supposed to date, you know?"

"No, I don't know." What kind of girl did that make me?

"She was a cheerleader at a school close by. She was bouncy and peppy… She thought she had all the answers… She didn't know anything."

"What didn't she know?" I was trying to figure it all out… I didn't want to make the same mistakes Kate did. I wanted to keep Scott, not push him away.

"She started finding out stuff about my family. She thought she could fix everything with a few brochures and self-help books. Life doesn't work that way."

"I guess…" Scott was right, I didn't want to hear anymore about his ex. I found myself wondering what she looked like… how pretty she probably was.

"Anyway…" I could tell that Scott sensed my mood. "It doesn't matter. You are the girl that's perfect for me. It's like we're puzzle pieces, you know?"

I blushed, "Yeah, I know."

He gave my forehead a peck. "See anything that peaks your interest?" He must've caught me taking another quick inventory of his room.

"So many books… Have you read all of them?"

"I guess so. There isn't much to do around here when Dad is home. I pretty much stay cloistered in my room. Can't bother him from in here…"

"Is it that bad? I mean... your dad?"

"He can be. It depends on the day." I was sorry to hear that. I had sort of been hoping that everything I had heard had been an exaggeration.

"Is that a picture of your mom?" I pointed to a small frame on his dresser. Inside the frame was a portrait of a beautiful woman. "She looks just like you." She had Scott's eyes and beautiful smile.

"Yeah, that was taken right after they got married; before she got pregnant." Scott got up and pulled another picture out of his top dresser drawer. He sat down next to me on the mattress and began carefully examining the photo; as if something in the photo might have changed since the last time he looked at it. "This one is of her and Dad."

"Wow... they look... I mean, they look happy." Their faces in the picture were nothing but smiles.

"I think they were. She was Dad's world, you know?" Scott's face never turned from the photo.

"Do you miss her? I mean, think of her a lot?"

"I miss not having a mom, I guess. I never knew her, so I can't say that I miss her, you know?" He touched her face gently with his fingers.

"What was her name?"

"Diane."

"Pretty name..." Scott got back up and placed the frame where it had been originally. "It is easy to see why your dad loved her so much." Scott quickly turned to face me. I could tell that I had gone too far. Mentioning his dad was not something I was generally allowed to do.

"So, Thanksgiving is next week... Big plans?" I was trying to steer the conversation in a different direction. I didn't want to upset Scott anymore than I already had.

"Yeah... Dad's going to make a turkey and a pie." His sarcasm was clear. "No plans."

"Come to my house." I hadn't asked my parents, but I didn't care. Thanksgiving wasn't my favorite holiday anyway. Having my parents mad at me wouldn't make that much of a difference.

"Thanks, but no."

"Seriously, you need to meet my family anyway."

"Arriving at your house for Thanksgiving would not be my ideal choice for meeting your parents for the first time." Scott's face showed his reluctance.

"Please come... you are the only thing I am thankful for..." The look in his eyes told me that I had won. I knew that I was fighting dirty, but this was important.

"It seems you have left me no choice. How can I say no to that?"

I smiled at him. For the first time in my life I was looking forward to Thanksgiving.

* * * * * * * * * * * * * * * * *

"You invited him to Thanksgiving?" Dad was not in immediate approval. "Why doesn't he want to spend the holiday with his own family?" I didn't want to go into Scott's family history with my father. That would only make matters worse.

"What does it matter? Instead of being at a table full of people I barely know and hardly like, I will have someone there to talk to."

"I don't like this... at all." Dad was looking at me over his glasses. He wasn't going to give up easily.

"Mom is already cooking a boatload of food. It isn't like there won't be enough to go around."

"It isn't fair to make that assumption. You should've cleared this with her first."

"If mom says it is okay…" Mom would say yes. She wouldn't like it, but her need to please everyone would force her to agree to my request.

"If your mother approves, then I guess it is okay." Dad went back to reading his paper.

Mom was in the kitchen cleaning up the mess that was left after dinner. I grabbed a towel and started helping with the dishes.

"What warrants this?" Mom wasn't stupid.

"Dad said I should ask you…" Mom didn't even look up from the sink. I could tell she was expecting the worst. "I invited Scott to Thanksgiving dinner."

Mom stopped washing the dish that she had been working on. She just stood there staring into the suds. I could hear her taking deep breaths. My guess was that she was counting to ten before speaking.

"So… that okay?" I knew I was pushing my luck. "He isn't picky or anything. I promise that we will stay out of everyone's way." I knew Mom hated Thanksgiving as well. Dad's family always came over for the holiday. None of them really got along creating a lot of tension during the day.

"Fine." I took it as a yes even though I knew she wasn't thrilled about it. I finished drying the dishes and went up to my room.

I couldn't wait to show Scott off to my family.

* * * * * * * * * * * * * * * * *

It smelled like Thanksgiving. I could smell the turkey and the potatoes. I knew that Mom always got up super early Thanksgiving morning to start the preparations for the big meal. I didn't know why she even bothered, no one really liked any of the food. All any of the relatives wanted to do was watch football. That was the only activity that was safe; no one would fight during the games.

Scott was supposed to arrive in a few hours. I couldn't wait. I knew that he would change my entire Thanksgiving experience. It wouldn't matter that my snobby cousins refused to speak with me or that my grumpy grandparents were making snide comments about my mother. All that mattered was that Scott was going to be there. Everyone was going to love him.

I heard Hallie throwing a fit because her boyfriend wasn't allowed to come over and mine was.

"So just because this is Sidney's first boyfriend she is allowed to do whatever?" I saw Mom struggle to keep it together. Trying to please everyone was extremely stressful.

"No, apparently Scott's family doesn't celebrate Thanksgiving and Sidney thought it would be nice to share our meal with someone less fortunate." Did Mom really just call Scott less fortunate?

"No Mom, Scott's family is just messed up. You should hear what..."

That was when I decided to interject. "What about Scott?"

Hallie just stared at me. She hadn't known that I was in earshot of their conversation. "It just isn't fair, that's all." Hallie knew it was a bad idea to go into the rumors surrounding Scott in front of me.

"Fine Hallie. You can invite your friend over after the meal. Okay? But I don't want to hear another word about it." Mom knew that her compromise would shut Hallie down. By that point Mom had just about all the she could handle.

Hallie took the hint and stormed to her room. I doubted very much that we would see her again before dinner. Even Hallie had a hard time swallowing the time spent with Dad's company.

I wanted Scott to arrive early. I wanted to make sure he beat all the relatives to the house. I sat in the front room all morning pretending to watch the Macys parade when in reality I was watching the window. The only thing that could calm my nerves would be to see his truck pull up.

As predicted, he arrived promptly. I watched him sit in his truck a few moments before heading to the door. I wished he wasn't so nervous. He was carrying a casserole dish. I was curious as to what he brought as I hadn't told him to bring anything. I didn't even know he could cook. I opened the door before he had a chance to ring the bell.

"Hey you…" I stepped up to him and kissed his cheek. He turned his face so that kissing his lips was not an option. Clearly he was nervous about meeting my parents and wanted to make a squeaky clean impression. "What did you bring?" I held out my hands to take the mystery dish.

"Um… Yeah, I thought I should bring something. It's green bean casserole. I hope that's okay. I didn't really know…" I had never seen Scott like this before. His voice was even shaking.

"You didn't have to… let's go take it back to the kitchen." I walked Scott back to where Mom was still slaving.

"Mom?" She looked up from the sweet potatoes. "This is Scott. He brought a casserole." Mom put on a good show. She smiled ear to ear.

"It is very nice to finally meet you. Thanks for the dish… does it need to go in the oven?"

"No ma'am. Well, maybe, but only to be warmed up."

"I will make sure it finds its way to the table. Sidney, why don't you offer your guest a drink or something to snack on?" My mother, Donna Reed.

"I'm fine thank you." Scott looked afraid to move.

"C'mon Scott. Let's go watch TV or something." I took his hand and led him out of the kitchen and into the living room to meet my father.

"Dad…" He didn't even look up from the paper. "This is Scott."

Dad lowered the paper a little so that he could take a good look and the Thanksgiving intruder. He tilted his head so that he was looking over his bifocals. "Good to meet you, Scott." With that Dad resumed reading his paper, or at least pretended to. It was clear that Dad had no desire to say anything more.

I took Scott upstairs to my room. "See, painless, right?"

"Not exactly." Scott's body seemed to relax a little once we were away from everyone. "I haven't had to meet parents before. One perk to not having girlfriends."

"You were great." I walked over to him and put my arms around his waist. He still seemed reluctant to show any sort of affection. "You okay?" I stepped back.

"This is your room... I mean, we are alone in your bedroom."

"And? We've been alone in your bedroom before."

"Yeah... that's different." I was beginning to feel very guilty for forcing Scott to come. It was becoming quite clear that he was extremely uncomfortable and that he longed to leave.

"You don't have to stay. I don't want you to be miserable all day. I'm sorry... I just thought..."

"It isn't that, Sidney. I'm just nervous. I just want everyone to like me, you know? I mean, this is your family. It's important that they approve. I don't want your dad thinking I'm up here taking advantage of you."

"I seriously doubt that's what he's thinking." I knew that Dad was most likely thinking about the best way to arrange the food on his plate during dinner.

"Hey Sidney?" Scott had a very confused look on his face. "What's going on with your room? I mean, you have been here awhile…" He was eyeing the strange arrangement of the furniture and the paint mess in the corner.

"Yeah… I sort of started this project and haven't gotten around to finishing it yet. I managed to find other ways to pass the time." I blushed. He knew that being with him was now how I chose to spend my time.

"Feel like finishing it up?" I was dumbfounded. He was serious.

"What? Now?"

"Sure, why not?" He started taking off his sweater leaving on only a white t-shirt.

"Because I'm a disaster, remember? I can't do anything without making a complete mess."

"Then we had better get started so that you have time to clean up before dinner." Scott grabbed a brush and had at it. I could tell that something about this project made him feel more at home. I wasn't sure if it was just something to keep him busy or if it was the feeling of helping me out. Either way, it helped him come out of his shell.

I heard my family start to arrive. It didn't matter. Scott and I were totally immersed in our project. Since no one bothered us I guessed that our presence wasn't missed. We were having a great time upstairs and I had no intention of stopping in order to talk to people that I didn't even like.

Scott painted more that half of the remaining pink walls without getting a single drop of blue paint on him. I didn't know how he did it. As promised, I was covered in it. I held a very strong resemblance to a smurf. There was paint in my hair, on my clothes, even under my fingernails. I wasn't sure how I was going to get it all off before the meal started.

"Girls! Dinner!" Dad yelled up the stairs.

Apparently I wasn't going to have time to get any of it off before dinner. I looked at Scott, "Are you ready?"

He was pulling his sweater back on. "I guess so."

Scott followed me downstairs.

"What have you done to yourself?" Mom looked pretty disgusted. Thanksgiving dinner was a formal affair.

Showing up wearing blue spots was not going to earn me any brownie points.

"Scott helped me finish painting my room."

"You had to do it today?" Mom's face was getting all pinched up. I wasn't scared though. I knew she wouldn't scream at me in front of everyone.

"Well, there was nothing else to do... Now I don't have to worry about it anymore." I just smiled at her. Nothing was going to ruin my day, not even my mother.

"At least try to get it all off of your hands," Mom quietly demanded before leaving to set up the remaining dishes for the big dinner.

The buffet was set up in the kitchen. Everyone was already helping themselves. I could see that Mom had set the formal dining room table. I was hoping that she would have split us up at smaller tables throughout the house so that Scott and I could hang out by ourselves. Now we were all going to have to eat together.

"Help yourself." I pushed Scott toward the spread of food. It was easy to tell which dish Scott had brought. His was the only one that actually looked good.

Scott took modest portions of everything. I could tell that he didn't want to insult my mother by not trying everything she had made.

"You don't have to eat all of it. I'm not." I only got a roll and some turkey. I hated dressing and stuffing along with anything coated in gravy.

"I'm fine. Don't worry about me."

I was glad to see that my family had been considerate enough to let Scott and I sit next to each other. That was more than I had expected of them.

The dinner conversation was primarily centered around my cousins. They both went to college at Purdue. My parents wanted to hear about every detail of college life, especially Dad. According to my dad, college years were the glory days. Hearing my cousins talk about classes and parties made my father's face light up. He was clearly living vicariously through them.

"So Scott, what are your plans?" My uncle Jerry, my dad's brother, asked Scott right as he was putting a forkful of food in his mouth.

Scott started chewing quickly so he could answer the question. I grabbed his hand under the table. It was easy to see that he was nervous. I was trying to help calm him down.

"My plans, sir?" Scott held his hand over his mouth as he was still working on his bite.

"After graduation? Haven't you decided where you're going yet?" Uncle Jerry was well aware that Scott wasn't going to college. Jerry just wanted to hear Scott say it out loud.

"I plan on staying here and helping Dad with the farm."

"Don't you need to study agriculture first?" My cousin Kyle was wearing a smirk with his question. They were just trying to rub it in, they were trying to make Scott feel bad and insignificant.

Scott started laughing. "I guess that might help some people, but I've been working that farm my whole life. I don't think spending a pile of money is going to help me figure out how to make the corn grow, do you?" I was impressed with Scott's answer and his attitude.

No one asked Scott for any more input. I gave him a big smile. I knew that he would make this the best Thanksgiving ever. He had just shut down my entire family. I had never been more proud.

As soon as the last fork had been put down I stood up to begin clearing the table. The sooner the mess was cleaned up the sooner everyone would leave. No one followed my lead. They just sat and watched me take their plates away. Scott noticed this as well. He stood up and began helping me. That only made me love him more. We carried the dishes into the kitchen.

"Let's get out of here," he whispered in my ear from behind me.

"Where can we go? Nothing's open."

"I have an idea." Of course he did… He wasn't going to have to twist my arm.

I peeked in at my family still sitting around the table. Dad was talking about something. Looked like everyone was going to be stuck there for awhile. I wrote a note and left it on the counter. Scott and I quietly snuck out the front door.

"I know just what you need," he winked at me. "Stress relief."

"Are you sure you're talking about me?"

He shrugged his shoulders. "Let's get some fresh air."

He pulled into the school parking lot. "We're here." He pointed to the track.

"It's locked. We can't get in."

"Sure we can." I followed him to the gate. He kneeled on one knee. "Put one foot on my leg and then step up to my shoulder. Pull yourself up and over from there. Think you can?"

"No, I will crush you."

"Doubtful. C'mon."

"Your bones…" I did exactly as he told me to. It took some effort getting over the top of the chain link fence, but I managed with some pushing power from Scott. "How are you going to…" I didn't need to finish my question. I watched him climb like a monkey up and over the gate. "Are you human?" He just laughed. "Now what?"

He walked up to the starting line. "I want to race you."

"Seriously?" This had to be about more than just racing. "You know I will beat you, right?"

"Let's find out." There was a look in Scott's eyes told me he wasn't kidding.

"Um… okay." I was glad I was still in painting gear and hadn't had a chance to get dressed up. Scott removed his nice sweater and threw it onto the bleachers.

"Don't let me win," he demanded. I nodded. I wouldn't. "Ready… Set… GO!"

It was harder to concentrate when running against Scott, especially since I felt like there was something wrong. I felt like he was trying to run away from something. There was a purpose to this, it didn't feel like it was just for fun. I still won, although not by as much as I should have. I hadn't really tried.

"What is going on? You don't even like to run." I had to know what was going through his head.

"Nothing." Scott wouldn't look at me. "Let's go again."

"No, not until you tell me the truth." I was determined.

"I just need to…" Scott crossed his arms in front of his chest. "I just need to get out some energy, that's all."

I understood. My family had bothered him more than he let on. He was mad. He was very mad. This was how he wanted to let it go. He just didn't want to tell me.

"Okay…. Let's go again." We kept running for hours. We changed the distances to mix it up. It felt good to run with him. The competition wasn't there. Neither of us cared who won or lost. This was about being together; letting go of our frustrations.

Finally, Scott stopped. "I think I'm done." We were both soaked with sweat. I could barely breathe anymore. My chest was heaving.

"Me too…" I hadn't wanted to admit it, but I had been done for awhile.

"Come sit with me." He grabbed my hand and took me into the middle of the field.

I laid down on my back. The ground was hard, but it felt good; cool. We just sat there, both of our bodies recovering.

"What do you want?" I turned my head to face him. "I mean, what do you dream about?"

"You mostly." He smiled.

"Seriously, how do you see your future?" I knew college wasn't where he was headed, but surely he had other things in mind.

"I just want to be happy, you know?" He kept staring into the sky. "I don't need much…"

"Do you see me?"

"I see you… kids… a house. I just want us to laugh a lot, to enjoy life together. I don't need a big house or fancy cars. I just…" He looked at me. I could feel what he meant. He didn't need to say anything else.

"My dad used to be happy… he loved my mom so much. Did you see that box of letters in my room?" I nodded yes. "Those are the letters they wrote to each other when he was stationed in Iraq before they got married. She was his life. Being away from her nearly killed him, more so than being in a war. It wasn't until I arrived that…" He stopped there. I didn't understand the guilt I heard in his voice. "His life ended when she died." He looked straight into my eyes. "He isn't crazy, Sidney… no matter what you have heard. He is just angry."

I didn't ask any questions. I let myself soak in the information that Scott willingly gave to me. He took my hand.

"I want to tell you something… But I can't yet, do you understand? I mean, I feel it, I really do, but…" His struggle for words told me what he wanted to say. Just knowing was all that I had longed for. I didn't need to hear anything, I just wanted to feel it.

"Me too." I squeezed his hand to show my understanding.

DECEMBER

Life with Scott only got better. Every moment I could spare was spent with him. Now that he had met my family, Scott wasn't afraid to come over. He came over every night after practice. My parents had requested that Scott leave every school night by eight. Saying goodbye to him was always the worst part of my day. He always called as soon as he got into his car to drive home. We would talk until he pulled into his driveway. Sometimes he would sit in his car and continue talking. Other times I could hear his dad yelling and Scott would have to let me go.

I still had yet to meet his father. Scott refused to let that happen. He told me there was no reason to introduce us. His dad was never sober long enough to have a real conversation. I didn't fight Scott on the issue. If he didn't want me to meet his dad, then I wouldn't.

My parents were sort of glad that I never went to Scott's house. That meant that we were always at my house. They liked being able to keep watch.

Dad never really spoke to Scott. Dad preferred to pretend that Scott didn't exist. Dad was constantly reminding me that I would be leaving soon for college and that I would meet all sorts of really great, educated people there. He meant boys. Boys from wealthy families. Boys who were studying to be doctors or lawyers. Not boys who were planning on staying in Wabash to run a farm.

Mom was much more accepting of Scott and his history as well as his potential future. She never once suggested that he and I break up. I didn't know what her true feelings were, but whatever they were she hid them very well.

* * * * * * * * * * * * * * *

"What do you want for your birthday?" Scott asked while trying to help me with my physics homework.

"That's a funny joke." I smiled as I looked up to meet his gaze.

"Seriously… it's coming up. What do you want?" Scott's persistence prevented me from ignoring the question again.

"My birthday is three days before Christmas… I don't get birthday presents." Usually my parents would buy one big item that was supposed to cover my birthday and Christmas. Relatives would just send one big box for the whole family to open on Christmas morning. My birthday presents would always be included in the mix.

"I want to do something nice for you for your big day."

"It isn't my 'big day.' Really…" I didn't want Scott to do anything for me. Just being with him was all I wanted.

"You leave me no choice." That was never a good thing to hear coming from him.

"Uh oh…"

"We have a date, officially, for December 22nd." I could see the wheels in his brain turning. The planning had already begun. Scott never did anything less than all-out.

"Do I need to wear formal attire?" I hoped that was taken as a joke.

"I can never get over your comedic talents."

There was no way that I was going to be able to concentrate on my physics homework after that. For the first time since I could remember I was excited about my birthday. I never minded that my birthday always seemed to get pushed aside, but I had to admit that it was sort of nice having someone care.

* * * * * * * * * * * * * * * *

"What would you like to do for your birthday?" It was like experiencing déjà vu, only with the wrong person. My mom had never before asked me that question. Usually she was too busy decorating the house or baking cookies to worry about what I wanted to do for my birthday.

"Um... I already have plans." Mom's reaction to my statement surprised me. She looked hurt, like I had taken something important away from her.

"This is your eighteenth birthday. It is a family affair. You can change your plans around."

"No I can't. And since when has my birthday ever been a big deal?" I was not going to let Mom ruin my day with Scott.

"Can I assume that your plans are with Scott?"

"Yes, you can." I was still shocked that we were even having this conversation.

"I don't like it. You spend every evening with him. You bring him over for Thanksgiving. And now you are letting him take this away from us." Mom's lips were pursed indicated how angry she was.

"Take what away from you? You never mentioned anything about wanting to do anything for my birthday. Plus, isn't it supposed to be my day? Meaning that I get to choose who I spend it with?" I could tell by her long pause that I was winning and she didn't like it.

"We are going to have a birthday dinner for you here on your birthday. You will be in attendance."

"And if I'm not?" I was turning eighteen, wasn't that supposed to mean I was free from their rules?

"I'm not giving you that option."

"Um… I think you sort of have to."

"Your father and I have something very special planned for you and you will be there. No questions."

"Then Scott will be there too." If she wanted me to be there she was going to have to compromise.

"What is it about him? Your father and I are starting to get worried that… Well, that he might not be the best thing for you." Where was this coming from?

"I'm not going to fight with you right now. Scott and I are a package deal. If you want me there, then you are going to have to settle for having the both of us." I left the kitchen and went straight out the front door. I wasn't going to give her an opportunity to strike back. The discussion was over.

* * * * * * * * * * * * * * * *

Scott had promised to go running with me during the holiday break. I couldn't afford my legs to get lazy and I dreaded running the distances alone, especially in the cold weather.

"We have to have dinner with my family on my birthday." I waited until we were at the halfway point of our run to bring it up. I was sort of hoping that he would be too tired to argue about it.

Scott stopped moving. I looked to my left and he wasn't there anymore. I turned around. He was standing behind me. He did not look happy.

"I'm not going to your house for dinner. I don't know if you remember the last time we tried that…" He didn't need to say anything else. The treatment he had gotten from my father and relatives had been inexcusable.

"This won't be like Thanksgiving, I promise. It will just be the five of us. You can wear anything you want, jeans are perfect. And it won't take nearly as long. It is just a formality, really…" I knew the whole ordeal would be miserable, but it would be worse if he wasn't there helping me along.

"Sid, I don't know… I can pick you up after, you know? It might be great that way. I will have more time to set up." Scott was trying hard to find a way out.

"You asked me what I wanted for my birthday…" I had him. I won. He couldn't turn me down.

He threw his head back in defeat. "What am I going to do with you?"

* * * * * * * * * * * * * * *

I could smell Mom cooking when I woke up. Surely she wasn't making anything that took this long to create for my birthday dinner. In my opinion, the longer something took to bake the worse it tasted. I truly would've been happy just ordering a pizza.

Since I knew the smell was for me and my special day I decided that I had better go downstairs and see what was going on.

"So, do you feel any older?" Mom was trying to hard to be chipper. I wondered how many cups of coffee she had already consumed.

"Sure thing." I sat on the stool by the counter. "What are you making?"

"Blueberry scones. I know they are your favorite."
I shot her a quizzical look. As far as knew, I had never had
a scone before.

"You really don't have to do this."

"How many times does a person turn eighteen?" By
this point I was almost grateful that my birthday had gone
unnoticed for so many years.

"Okay, you win." I would let her have this one.
"What time do the festivities start? I need to let Scott know
when to be here."

Her mood shifted slightly. "I was thinking dinner
would start around 6ish."

"Can we make it 5ish? Scott has something planned
for after…" She didn't like my question, I could tell.

"I suppose." She returned to her scones. As I
watched her make them I became more certain that I had
never tried one before. They looked like really hard rolls. I
would have much rather had a frozen waffle or something.
I felt guilty for thinking that knowing how hard she was
working, but then again, I hadn't asked for any of it.

"Where's Hallie?" I thought it best to change the
subject.

"Still in bed I guess."

"Um… Mom? Hallie didn't come home last night. She's not in her room." I hadn't mentioned it yet because I figured that she had just spent the night at a friend's house.

Mom dropped her spoon and ran upstairs like she didn't believe me. It took her thirty seconds to race downstairs and call Dad at the office. I couldn't hear what she was saying. Her next phone call was to the police.

I got up from my stool and grabbed my phone.

"Hi, Scott? Guess what? Looks like there's no family dinner tonight after all."

* * * * * * * * * * * * * * * *

By the time Scott arrived at my house there was a full blown search party. The police were there trying to create a timeline of places Hallie had last been seen. Mom had called all of Hallie's friends. They all, of course, supposedly hadn't seen her since the day before. It wasn't surprising that Hallie's phone was either dead or turned off; no matter the cause, it kept going straight to voicemail.

"Are you okay?" Scott wrapped his arms around me.

"Yeah… I guess." I didn't know why, but I wasn't really worried about her. I figured she had done something stupid and was afraid to come home. I knew she would show up sooner or later, I was just irritated that it happened on my birthday.

The police informed my parents that there was nothing left for them to do but wait. It was best if we stayed at the house just in case Hallie tried to call or came home. The clock moved slowly. I felt myself staring at the digital numbers willing them to change. We all sat in silence. Scott was next to me holding my hand. The longer she was gone the harder it was not to care.

"I'm sure she's fine…" Scott was trying to be a comfort, but I didn't want to talk about it. I just looked at him and nodded.

The day was passing. Minutes turned into hours. Hallie was still gone. I put my head between my knees. This was a new feeling for me. I felt sick. What if something really was wrong? Hallie thought I hated her. I didn't hate her, she was my sister. What if she was stuck in someone's basement? Horrid thoughts began flowing through my head.

The light in the room was changing as the sun moved through the sky. Over half the day was gone. Mom was sitting almost comatose on the couch. Dad kept pacing through the hallways. He was constantly on his cell phone trying to reach someone, anyone for an update. No one knew anything.

Finally, it became dark outside. Still no sign of Hallie. I tried to remember the last thing I had said to her. It was probably something obnoxious and hateful.

We all jumped when the phone rang.

"Hello?" Dad's voice was quivering. I couldn't tell what the voice on the other side of the line was saying. Dad's expression wasn't giving any clues. "Thank you." Dad hung up the phone.

"The police are on their way with her." Dad was looking at Mom.

"Where was she?" Mom sounded weak and tired.

Dad took a deep breath before speaking. "They found her and her boyfriend in an old abandoned barn on the south end of town. There had clearly been a party last night and Hallie had too much…" Dad looked down at his feet. This was the sort of trouble they had been trying to avoid by moving away from Chicago.

"You mean Hallie got drunk last night and has been puking all day in some barn?" I was furious. In my head I took back all the regrets I had been thinking.

"Looks that way, yes." I was amazed at how calm Dad seemed.

I saw headlights pull into the driveway.

"Seems like you were worried about the wrong boyfriend, huh?" I wasn't going to stick around for the show. I still had a little bit of birthday left and I didn't want to waste it watching Hallie get yelled at. "Let's go Scott."

"Where are you going?" Mom sounded desperate.

"Don't worry Mom, I'm not Hallie." Scott and I quickly left passing Hallie on the way in. She looked green. The cop was practically holding her up.

"Where do you want to go?" Scott asked after we got into his truck.

"I thought you had something special planned…"

"I do, I just wasn't sure if you were still in the mood. You know, it hasn't been a great day…." I felt bad that Scott had to sit through the drama with my family, but I had been grateful that he was there.

"Hallie's fine, that's all that really matters." I looked out the window. I wondered if she even cared about how much she had destroyed for me today.

"Well, I do have something planned, but it isn't much."

"I have no doubt it's perfect." I looked around the inside of his truck. There was nothing that I could tell that provided any clues as to what the surprise was.

Scott pulled up to the beach, the same beach where we had gone for the bonfire so many months ago. "Wait here."

It was dark so it was hard to tell was Scott was doing. He fished around the cab of the truck for a few minutes. It didn't take any time for him to start up a fire in the huge pit. He was on the other side of the flames making it impossible for me to see the set up. I couldn't help but smile. I could tell this was going to be great. Even after the events of the day, this would still be the best birthday ever.

He came to my side of the truck. "All ready." He helped me out. "Watch your step."

It was cold outside, but the heat from the fire made it seem quite warm. As we approached the bonfire I could see what Scott had done. He had laid out a blanket for us to sit on so that we could lean back onto the giant logs. I noticed a bag of hotdogs and a bag of marshmallows.

"You hungry?" Scott looked very proud of his work. It was simple, but it was exactly what I wanted. Scott knew me. He knew I didn't want jewels or other expensive presents. All I wanted was time with him.

"You bet." I watched Scott as he unfolded a couple of coat hangers. He forced a hotdog onto each of them. There we sat, together, roasting hotdogs over an open fire.

"Do you know why I picked hotdogs?"

"Because they are easy?"

Scott started laughing. I immediately had a hunch as to what he was about to say. "Because I am dying to see you stick half of it in your mouth again the way you did at Homecoming." I felt my face flush. There was no way that I was going to be able to deny him his one request.

"Okay, but only if you brought buns." Scott magically produced another bag containing buns from behind his back.

I took my cooked hotdog and stuck in a bun. Scott was staring at me smiling in anticipation. There was no way out of it... I crammed more than half of it into my mouth. I felt like a chipmunk. My cheeks were stretched to their max. Scott started rolling on the ground. If that was all it took to make him happy, then I was glad to oblige.

He sat up and kissed my still chubby cheeks. "That was exactly what I wanted. Thank you!"

130

I tried to reply but couldn't due to the incredibly large mass of food still stuck in my mouth. I was having a hard time getting it all to go down.

"Ready for a marshmallow?" I had to nod yes as I was still working on the hotdog.

Using the same coat hangers he put two marshmallows on the ends of each one. It only took seconds for them to catch on fire cooking them to perfection.

"Do you remember how to eat these?"

"Yes, all at once. Don't bite into it." Even I had to smile at that memory. It had been like a waterfall of white goo spilling all over me.

"Want to know why I brought the marshmallows?" Scott wasn't laughing anymore.

"Because they go well with hotdogs?"

"Because watching you make a mess last time was when I knew I was in trouble." Scott leaned in closer. "That's when I knew you weren't someone I was going to be able to get rid of." He kissed me softly.

I didn't know how to respond. His words were all the present that I ever wanted. Just knowing that he cared was the perfect gift.

"I have one more thing for you." Scott reached behind one of the large logs.

"Seriously, you have already done too much…" Before I had a chance to stop him he placed a simply wrapped box in my lap.

"Don't get too excited. It isn't diamonds or anything."

I carefully peeled back the paper. I wanted to make the whole experience last as long as possible. I opened the white box. Inside was a beautiful wooden frame holding a picture of Scott and me. "Where did this picture come from?"

"Emily took it at the bonfire. I think it's great…" The picture was perfect. The photo was of Scott holding me in his arms. We were facing each other and smiling; as if nothing else existed. The picture somehow seemed to capture the definition of our relationship.

"Scott… this is…" I held the picture to my heart. "This is perfect."

My reaction seemed to be what he had been hoping for. He wrapped his arm around my shoulders. "It just looks like us, don't you think?" I nodded.

We sat for awhile in silence just watching the fire. I felt safe with him. He was my home. He was my family.

"You think Hallie's okay?" His question surprised me. I didn't want to talk about her, not now.

"Stupid, but okay."

"What're your parents going to do?"

"Probably nothing. They're just glad she's home. She looked pretty bad walking into the house, did you see her?"

"I wasn't paying much attention. I've dealt with my share of drunks…" I hadn't given much thought to the fact that this had been familiar territory for Scott. "Do you drink?" I sensed the seriousness of his tone.

"Never." I wasn't lying.

"Not at all? Why?"

"Because of what happened to Hallie. It makes people stupid. I do enough dumb things on my own… I don't need any help." I started writing in the sand with a stick I had found. My anti-drinking philosophy had never earned me any friends in the past. I wasn't sure what Scott's take on it would be.

He smiled. "Good. I don't deal well with alcohol or the people who choose to drink it."

"Can we change the subject?" The mood had gotten too serious for me.

Scott looked and me and smiled. He put his arm over my shoulder and pulled me closer to him. We returned to sitting in silence.

I picked up the picture that Scott had given to me. I traced his face with my fingers. I could see the adoration in my eyes when looking at him and that was after only a few days. Since then he had become my life, my reason for breathing. I wondered if that could be captured in a photograph.

JANUARY

The snow finally came. I had seen snow before, but I had lived in the city. Streets were always cleared and it seemed like the snow turned to sludge instantly. I hadn't been exposed to what snow could really look like.

Scott hadn't been able to take me back to the trestle at all once the snow arrived. The snow came up to my knees when we tried to walk through the field. I missed it. I was dying to see what it looked like covered with the blanket of white.

"Can you handle cold weather?" Scott asked me once while we were watching a movie at my house.

"Um… I guess so. You mean colder than this?"

"I mean, do you mind being outside for periods of time when the weather is like this?" He pointed out the window. Even though I was toasty warm cuddled up to Scott, just looking outside made me shiver. The sky looked gray and everything was coated with a layer of ice.

"I guess it would depend on what the reward was for suffering so…" I had zero desire to play in the snow. Being cold and wet was not something I was interested in.

"What if I promised to warm you up after?" He began softly kissing my neck. How could I possibly say no to an offer like that?

"Then I guess I am game. What do you have planned?"

"Secret. I will let you know soon enough." At that point we resumed watching the movie. Both of my parents were home and no part of the house was sound proof. I was certain that Hallie had her hears pressed against the other side of the wall hoping to hear something that could be used against me and Scott.

* * * * * * * * * * * * * * * *

It was a Thursday night. The snow started to fall right around ten. The flakes were enormous. It was like cotton falling from the sky. Everything was coated. I was in bed when I heard the tapping on my window. The sound initially startled me as it woke me from a very real dream. I was dreaming about Scott. About Scott's skin on my skin. About his hands on my body. About his lips exploring. That was something I was very much anticipating, but had yet to experience.

I got out of bed and walked to the window. Even though it was late at night, all the snow made everything brighter. It made the sky appear to be almost purple. I could see him despite the snow falling. He was standing a few feet from the house under my window. He looked amazing, almost as if he was glowing. I knew that he could see me.

I immediately became acutely aware that my hair was probably all over the place and that I was only wearing a t-shirt that was practically worn through. To be fair, I hadn't expected company. We had already said our daily goodbye hours ago.

Scott waved for me to come down. Without a second thought I quickly dressed and darted as quietly as possible down the stairs. I grabbed my coat and was out the door.

"It's snowing!" Scott said it as if I was not capable of seeing the flakes for myself.

"Yeah…." Did he come all the way out here to give me a weather report?

"You ready?"

"For what?"

"To take a ride.."

"As long as it is with you, then yes, I'm ready." I knew this was going to be great.

We hopped into the truck and were off. Scott was forced to drive slowly as the streets were far from being cleared.

"Where are we going?" I ask with controlled excitement.

"Secret…"

"You love secrets." I smiled. Never once had he disappointed me with one of his surprises.

We were driving down a now familiar road. I knew where we were. We were headed toward his farm. The snow was falling hard, it made seeing out the windshield difficult. It didn't seem to bother Scott. He knew these roads.

Instead of pulling off to the side of the road as we would have if we were headed to the trestle, Scott turned onto a gravel drive. I was sure he was driving us to his house.

"Stay here. I'll be right back." Scott disappeared behind the house. A few moments later I heard the sound of a very large motor. Something I might have earlier described as an alien spacecraft of sorts was headed directly for me. I was tempted to jump out of the truck and run; however, I knew that Scott was driving whatever that contraption was.

It was the largest tractor I had ever seen. I didn't know how he thought I was going to climb onto it. I had never been on a tractor before. He jumped down from the driver's seat like he was Spiderman.

"C'mon!" He pulled me out of the truck.

"How am I supposed to get up there?" I wasn't a mountain climber… Scott climbed up first. Then, he grabbed my hands and pulled me up as I tried to negotiate a foot pattern. Before I knew it I was sitting next to him, my favorite spot in the world.

Without saying a word Scott began to drive. The snow didn't seem to bother the tractor. I was certain that it could have driven through anything. The fields looked spectacular. It was like riding on top of a cloud. Finally we approached the edge of the woods. I knew where he wanted to take me.

Walking through the woods was not as difficult as hiking through the fields as the trees prevented the snow from getting as deep as it did in the clearing. It was magical. I felt corny for thinking that, but there was no other way to describe it. It was like something out of a dream. Then, we were there.

Seeing our place covered in white was nothing like I had imagined… it was so much more. I didn't want to ruin this moment with words. Scott must have felt the same way, for he also said nothing. Instead, he just held my hands in his. The snow was falling all around us. It didn't matter. It was the most beautiful thing I had ever seen. The snow illuminated everything. It emitted a feeling of warmth; like a big white blanket draped over everything. I no longer noticed the cold.

Scott just looked at me.

"I want to tell you something... But, I don't want you to say anything tonight, deal? I mean you can talk… I just don't want you to feel obligated…" He seemed nervous.

"Okay…."

"I don't read romance novels or watch mushy movies. So, I'm sorry if I don't do this right." I just stared at him. He couldn't look at me. He wouldn't look at me. "Sidney, I love you. I mean I am in love with you. I have wanted to tell you for so long… I didn't want to say anything until I knew for sure… that it was real. You deserve so much… I had to make it special, you know?" I nodded. I felt tears fall down my face. I couldn't help it. Hearing those words…

He wiped away my tears with his sleeve. He pulled me to him and kissed me. I felt his embrace get stronger, as if this was the last time he would ever have this opportunity. I kissed him back… I held his face in my hands. I kissed his neck. My hands held onto the back of his coat. If I could have somehow molded our bodies together I would have.

It was always him that had to gently take the step back, to slow things down. I was glad that he had the strength to do that. If it were up to me, we would have been permanently bound together.

"I should get you back home. Your parents don't even know you are gone." He was right, although I hated to admit it.

We made the trek back to the tractor and again were driving, only this time back to his house.

"I am surprised the engine didn't wake up your dad.. I mean, it is so loud!" I had to yell to make sure I was heard.

"He started drinking pretty early today. He passed out long before I went to pick you up. Once he is out, there is no waking him. Anyway, he is like a grizzly being woken too early if forced up. He is better just left alone." That was more than he had ever said about his father. Normally his dad was a subject that wasn't brought up.

Scott went ahead and pulled the tractor into the barn with me still on it. No sense in dropping me off at the truck. I had already had my surprise.

"What the hell do you think you're doing?" The strange voice was rough and quiet. There was anger in his words. It was clear that he never had to yell to instill fear within his audience.

I jumped in my seat. I hadn't expected anyone to be waiting for us. He was standing in the shadows, as if intentionally hiding. I had never seen him before, the infamous Max Andrews. He was a giant of a man. It looked like he hadn't shaved in weeks. He was not the same man I had seen in the photo Scott showed me.

He was carrying a bottle of whiskey in one hand and a cigarette in the other. I wondered how long he had been waiting in the barn for us.

"Sidney, go to the truck…" Scott wasn't asking me, he was telling me. "Now." I scrambled down my side of the tractor. I was afraid to leave the barn as I didn't want to walk any closer to where his dad was.

"You didn't answer my question." Max Andrews was gradually getting louder and closer. I was officially scared. I could smell the alcohol. He reeked.

"Just went for a ride, nothing criminal." Scott answered. His glib attitude seemed to turn a switch inside his father. Scott turned his back on his father for just a second, if that, to make sure I was okay.

I saw it happen. I watched as Mr. Andrews raised the bottle over Scott's head. I screamed, "Stop!" But nothing came out. Scott turned around just as the bottle came crashing down. Scott was able to get somewhat out of the way, but the bottle still landed on his shoulder.

I ran to him. Blood was everywhere. He needed stitches. Color drained from his face. He was struggling to stay on his feet. I knew Scott didn't want his father to see him fall.

I watched as Mr. Andrews calmly threw the remainder of the broken glass bottle down on the ground. He looked over his shoulder, "Take the girl home." He then walked straight into the house without so much as glancing back.

This was my nightmare. I had seen it in my dreams. But this wasn't a dream. This was real. The fear was real. As soon as his father was in the house Scott submitted to the pain. He fell to the ground grasping his shoulder trying to hold the pieces of his loose skin together.

"Oh my god… you're bleeding..." I tore off my coat and began using it to help soak up the blood, to get a better idea as to what the damage was.

"I'm fine, really." He didn't look or act fine.

"You need a doctor. We need to call the police." I was frantic. I didn't know what to do. Scott was hurt, badly. I couldn't even finish my own thoughts. I just kept seeing the bottle strike Scott over and over in my head. I should've stopped him. I should've gotten to Scott faster. "I'm so sorry…."

"This is not your fault… Don't think that for a second." I thought I saw tears in Scott's beautiful eyes. My heart was breaking. I wanted to make this better but I didn't know how.

Scott grabbed onto me with his good arm. "Sidney…I need you to calm down."

He was so much braver than I was. The snow started coming down even thicker than before. A blanket of snow had already started to cover the floor of the barn. The snow was no longer a beautiful white. Instead, it was the color of red velvet. I couldn't get the bleeding to stop. Scott's face was turning pale. He once pink lips were starting to look blue. His eyes had lost their sparkle.

The cut was bad. Just by looking at it I could see pieces of glass in the wound. It looked like his skin had been shredded away from his body. From somewhere within himself Scott gathered the strength to sit up. He managed to peel away what was left of his shirt. He examined the wound. He began picking the pieces of glass out one by one.

"There is super glue on the counter on the back wall. Will you go get it?" Did he really just ask me for super glue? I didn't question him out loud; I just did as he asked.

The last time I saw him shirtless was the day he saved me from drowning. I was too far away from him then to really take a good look. Seeing him this time did not have the same effect. There he was, sitting amongst the now red snow with nothing covering the top half of his body. I could see now... there were scars all over him. Not clean, straight scars that might result from surgery... these were angry scars. Some were worse than others, but they were all there. There were too many to ignore.

"Are all of these from your dad?" After hearing the question Scott just sat there silently removing what was left of the glass. He gave me a look that let me know the answer to my question was yes.

"Hand me the super glue..."

I watched as he literally glued his body back together. This was clearly not his first time doing this. The glue seemed to work. Scott sat there holding the pieces of his skin together as the glue dried. The flow of blood subsided.

"Come on... let's get out of the cold. You have to be freezing..." I helped him up. We walked back to the truck. He didn't argue when I got in the driver's seat. He laid his head down on my lap. I covered him with the blanket that he always kept behind the seat. I turned the key and let the engine roar to life. It took awhile for the heat to kick in, but it was a warm relief when it did. Scott finally stopped shivering. I ran my fingers through his hair. Up and down his back. Finally, he let it out… I felt him crying. His whole body was shaking. His sobs were coming uncontrollably. I had no idea how long all of this had been bottled in. How much had he kept inside himself, afraid to show anyone?

I just continued to try and comfort him. No words. The tears eventually began to slow down. I couldn't see his face. All I knew was that his body was no longer convulsing. I thought maybe he had fallen asleep.

I was unaware of time. I had no idea how long we sat in the truck. Inevitably, the truck stopped running. It had run out of gas.

"There's gas in the barn." Scott slowly got out and walked to get the gas. His body disappeared in the snowstorm. Even though I knew he was okay, I still felt myself getting nervous when I could no longer see him.

My eyes didn't leave the barn. Seconds felt like eternity. I knew his father was still in the house, but I couldn't help but be scared. Relief filled me when I saw him carrying the container of gas. I was also glad to see that he had found a flannel jacket in the barn as well.

"Scoot over. I don't want you to drive in this…"
His voice had a quality in it that I didn't recognize. I knew
that we had crossed a line tonight.

I waited until we hit a paved road before I chose to
say anything.

"How often does this happen?" I paused… "I mean,
I saw the scars."

"It depends. Drinking always makes it worse.
Usually if I can manage to stay out of his way…" His mind
seemed to wander to a far away place. "I really thought he
would sleep through the tractor."

"Shouldn't we call the police or something?"

"No… never." He stared right at me. "I mean it.
Never." His message was clear. I was not to mention this
to anyone.

"Okay, but why? Why do you let him do that to
you?"

"Let him? I don't just let him… You wouldn't
understand."

"I can try, if you tell me." I knew he wouldn't. His
tone told me he was done talking about it. "Scott… how
did your mom die?" After seeing his dad in action

tonight... The thought of his dad as a murderer wasn't an unrealistic one.

At first he didn't say anything. He just drove. I could tell this wasn't something he was ready to talk about.

"All I know is what I was told. I was too young to remember..."

"What were you told?"

"Dad told me everything, so I can't promise it is totally accurate. According to him, Mom never was quite right after she had me. Depression or something... Dad came home from the fields one day and found her in the bathtub. She had taken one of his razors and cut her wrists. She didn't do it right... I guess it took her hours to bleed out. If Dad would've gotten home sooner she could've been saved, no problem. Dad said I watched the whole thing happen from my crib. I didn't even cry, at least that's what he says..." I wasn't sure how to respond. Now I knew why Scott took whatever his dad handed out; Scott felt responsible for the death of his mother which is what ultimately broke his father.

"I don't date because eventually all this stuff comes out. How long could I have hidden my dad from you? How long before you found out about Mom? People hear this and they look at me different, like I'm a lost puppy or something." It made sense. I can't say that I wouldn't have tried to shut people out as well under those circumstances.

"Scott… I don't care about your history. I don't care where you think your future is going. The only thing in this whole world that matters to me is you. I get it… But, I don't care." He still couldn't look at me.

I cuddled up into him as he drove. I had no idea what time it was. It was still dark, but Wabash was always dark this time of year. I was just hoping that everyone at home was still in bed. I didn't want to answer any questions about my night.

I knew we were getting close to my house.

"I will see you tomorrow?" I felt like we were breaking up or something. Like I had seen too much…

"No…" He looked right at me as he said it. "You will see me later today." He flashed me his beautiful smile. With one last hug and kiss we said good bye. I went inside and watched from the window as he drove away while the tears streamed down my face.

* * * * * * * * * * * * * * * *

"I heard you leave…. That was quite some time ago. I guess I needn't ask who you were with." My mom spoke calmly, although I was anxious to see what her real reaction to my absence was. I wasn't sure how much more drama I could handle.

"Look… Not now, please?" I was hoping that she would let this go. After all, I did come home, and safely at that.

"Was it Scott? That you left with?"

"Yes."

"You thought it was okay to go out in the middle of the night? That no one would notice?" I couldn't tell where this was going. She didn't seem mad…

"Yeah… it wasn't a big deal. Besides, I have never done anything to make you think I am irresponsible or untrustworthy." I tried to abruptly end the conversation by heading up the stairs.

"We aren't done…"

"Why? Why aren't we done? Because you need to know every detail of how I spent the last few hours? We didn't have sex if that is what you are thinking…" I heard myself say it. I could tell I had made the conversation even that more awkward.

"I am glad to know that… but that wasn't my concern." I followed her into the kitchen. I watched her pour another cup of coffee. "Have a seat." She motioned for me to sit down next to her. At this point it was going to be easier to comply. My actions warranted consequences, I knew that.

"Sidney, I was afraid you weren't coming back. I see the way you and Scott are together. It is almost as if you are one person living in two bodies." I felt my face flush. How was I supposed to respond to this. I was exhausted. I knew that Mom had no idea of what I had already gone through today, but... I just didn't have it in me to fight right now. I felt like all the life in me had been sucked out. "Are you planning on leaving, permanently? With Scott I mean?"

"No... I have college and he... well, he has the farm."

"Have you made any decisions about college?"

"Mom, I am really tired. Is this what you really want to talk about, college? Because that might be able to wait until tomorrow."

"I just want to make sure you are thinking with your head. Scott is great, we all think so. But he isn't everything. There are a lot of people out there that you have never met. You are still so young...So much ahead of you." So these were Mom's true feelings. She felt the same way as Dad.

The farmer wasn't good enough for their little girl. What was good enough? Money? Cars? When did a person's heart no longer become a part of the equation?

"I will take your words into consideration…" That was all I could think to say.

"He is your first boyfriend… "

"That matters because…."

"There are a lot of nice guys out there, he isn't the only one."

"Can I go to bed now?" I couldn't do this anymore. I wanted to scream at her. She knew nothing about Scott. No one did. Who was she to pass judgment?

"This is between us. I won't tell your father. Just please, don't make this a habit."

I nodded my head and left for my bedroom. Seeing Scott at my window seemed like a hundred years ago. So much had happened in such a small amount of time. Now I knew I loved Scott. This wasn't a crush. This wasn't merely lust. This was the die-for-you kind of love that I had only heard about in movies. In my head and my heart I knew that there was no one else I could ever possibly feel this way about.

FEBRUARY

Scott and I did not talk about that night in January. We both tried to act as if it had never happened. That wasn't terribly difficult as Scott refused to discuss any topic that was remotely related to any member of his family. There were times when I would notice a fresh wound. He never said anything, but I was sure they were from his dad.

I knew that I couldn't protect him from his father, but I could make our time together as special as possible.

College was still an issue. I had been accepted at both IU and Purdue. Staying in Indiana was no longer, obviously, a problem for me. I knew Scott wasn't going anywhere. After graduation he would officially take over the farm. At least if I stayed close to home we would have a chance to see each other, even if only on the weekends.

Talking about college only angered Scott. I brought up the possibility of attending a commuter college so that I could live at home, that way we could still see each other every day. Scott insisted that I was being ridiculous. He didn't want to me to sacrifice my education for him. It got to the point that we had to stop bringing it up altogether. Just thinking about the separation made me physically ill.

Dad was pushing me to make a decision. Mom didn't say anything, but I knew it was stressing her out. Hallie was just waiting for me to leave so that she could claim some of my closet space for her own.

I just wasn't ready. All I wanted, all I needed, was Scott. I had to find a way for us to stay together. Four years might as well have been all eternity. It was next to impossible for me to make it through the day without him… how was I supposed to make it through a week? A month? I just couldn't let myself focus on that.

"If you were going to college in the fall, what do you think you would study?" Scott and I were in my room trying to finish up homework. I was having a difficult time concentrating as I was staring at a college visitation form that my dad had handed me earlier that evening. I was going to have to at least go and visit; talk to some people.

Maybe that would buy me some time before having to make any final decisions.

"Um... Agriculture, I guess..." Scott didn't even look up from his book.

"Well... that's not going to work." I had planned on visiting IU and they didn't have an agriculture program. "How about top two?"

"What are you doing?" Scott scooted closer to me so that he could see what I was working on. "What is that?"

"We are going to visit IU in a couple of weeks and I need to have an area of interest picked out."

"We?"

"Yes. You and I are going to Bloomington to check things out."

"Were you planning on asking me first?" I could sense Scott's hesitation.

"Well... I'm asking you now. Will you please go with me? We don't have to stay long. I just need to get some signatures from the admissions office for proof. It's a free day out of school... college visitation and all..."

"Why are you asking me what I want to study? Shouldn't this be about you?"

"I have no idea what I want to do." How was I, at the age of eighteen, supposed to pick out what I wanted to do for the rest of my life?

"What are you choices?"

"Anything... except agriculture." I smiled at him.

"Just pick something general... like business or... science."

"Have you seen my science grades? Really not going to happen. Business is okay though. How hard can that be?" I completed the rest of the form easily. I was delighted that Scott hadn't put up too much of a fight about going. Having him around always made everything more endurable.

* * * * * * * * * * * * * * *

"Do you even know how to get there?" Scott asked after pulling out of my driveway.

"Sort of... They sent me a map of where to go." It had been a struggle to get my parents to allow me to visit IU without them but instead with Scott. But, at least I was going, and that was something just in itself.

The drive to Bloomington was just under three hours from my front door.

"So… what are you planning on majoring in?" Scott asked while in route.

"I don't know." I tried not to think about it.

"Well, what are you good at? What do you like doing?"

"Nothing… running." I shrugged my shoulders. My list of talents was a short one. I wasn't a great student. I didn't communicate well. I definitely was not interested in the arts. My only shining moments were when I was on the track.

"Can't you major in sports or something?" I knew Scott was only trying to be helpful, but just thinking about it made my stomach turn in knots.

"I'm not good at sports. I'm only good at running. You can't major in running." I was hoping that he would sense my tone.

"What about Sports Medicine or Physical Therapy?"

"Scott, I don't want to talk about this anymore." I turned my head to face out the window. Leaving Scott wasn't the only reason I was avoiding the topic of college. I was scared. I wasn't good with anything unfamiliar. I had been in Wabash for months now and still didn't really have any friends other than Scott.

"Okay... Sorry." I hadn't meant to be short with him; he just kept pushing the issue.

The remainder of the drive was a quiet one.

As soon as the truck was parked we were greeted by IU tour guides. I instantly felt as if we were a part of a large herd of cattle. We were told where to sit, when to stand, where to walk to... The entire cattle drive experience pretty much ruined the college tour. I got the impression that Scott felt the same way; although, he didn't say anything negative. In fact, he really didn't say anything at all.

After the large group activities were over Scott and I were told to walk over to the School of Business as I had chosen that as my area of interest. The man in charge of admissions to the business program handed me a very thick folder and starting rambling on about classes, coursework, and overall responsibilities of and expectations from students. I didn't pay much attention as it didn't take long for me to determine that this was not the route I was going to take.

"Do you have any questions for me?"

"Yes. Will you please sign this for me?" I smiled as I slid the visitation form across the table. I needed his signature as proof that I had, in fact, visited campus. His expression told me that he and I were on the same page as to my entrance into the world of business. As soon as his pen left the paper Scott and I were off.

Our duties as far as IU was concerned were officially over. "What now?" Scott looked at me for directions.

"I don't know… We could head home I guess." I didn't really see a reason to stick around Bloomington any longer than necessary.

"We drove all the way here… Surely there is something fun for us to do." Scott walked over to a bulletin board decorated with very colorful fliers. "Look. There's all kinds of stuff going on."

"But we're not students here. I don't think anyone wants us to crash their party."

"Not all of it is for students. There is a housing fair in Alumni Hall… We could try to get tickets to a basketball game." Scott's eyes must've found something really interesting because he stopped talking. He just stared at the board for a few seconds. I tried to guess which flier he was studying, but there were too many to tell. "I've got it… let's go." His smile indicated that he had found something brilliant. He had never disappointed me thus far, so I took his hand and simply followed his lead.

I didn't know how Scott knew where he was going. I didn't question him as his confidence told me he knew exactly where he was. We ended up in front of what looked to be a very old building. It was huge. I was afraid to go inside.

"Are you sure this is the right place?" I felt bad asking, but it didn't feel right.

"I have no doubt." He took me inside the main door. He just stood in the entrance tilting his head from side to side as if trying to listen for something. He must've heard what he was listening for because he grabbed my hand and starting pulling me down the hallway.

I quickly began to hear music. It wasn't a song I was familiar with. There were no words, but there was a very strong beat. I couldn't place the genre.

We arrived at the room where the music was originating from.

"This is a ballroom dancing class, isn't it?" I looked at Scott. He was beaming.

"It's great, right?" He squeezed my hand.

"Ballroom dancing, really?" I had never danced like that before. It didn't appear to be a beginner's class either. All the couples were doing steps that I was sure would cause me many broken bones.

"C'mon." H walked into the room. I hesitated. "C'mon!" He tugged on my arm.

Before I had a chance to say no we were approached by what seemed to be an instructor. She smiled, "Are you here to dance?" Scott quickly nodded his head. She took both of our hands and led us onto the floor. She arranged our arms so that we were in proper form. She must've sensed my apprehension. She stood behind me and placed one hand on each hip. I could feel her dancing behind me. I was shocked at how well Scott was doing not to mention how much fun he thought it was. I felt awkward and clumsy. I knew I didn't look as graceful as the other girls in the room. They seemed to be floating on top of the floor while I felt like I was clomping my feet down with each step.

The instructor stayed with us for two songs. My lack of enthusiasm must've pushed her away, either that or my complete lack of talent.

"Aren't you having fun?"

"Um… I'm not very good at this." I hated to disappoint him, but I didn't want to stay any longer.

"Sure you are." Scott's encouragement wasn't helping.

"I'm not…" I looked down at the floor. I was too ashamed to tell him how badly I felt about myself at that moment.

"Alright… let's go." The relief was instant.

We started to walk back to the car. I was so glad that the day was almost over. This place was not for me. I could tell. The idea of it… of having to live in this crowded campus full of people I didn't know… It terrified me. I could feel my hands becoming clammy just at the thought.

"Why were you so miserable back there?" Scott's question told me that he had wanted to stay longer. His disappointment showed.

I just shook my head. I didn't want to talk about it. I was too embarrassed as it was.

"Seriously, talk to me…" Scott stopped walking and turned to face me. "You can tell me…"

We were standing outside in front of a large fountain. It was freezing and the snow had started to fall.

This was not where I wanted to have this conversation. I kept walking.

"Sidney, stop." He grabbed my arm. "What's going on in there?" He tapped his finger on my head.

"Scott... I'm not good at anything. I can't even..."

"Is that what this is about? Dancing?"

I nodded yes. I looked away from him. I hated having him see me like this.

"I don't care if you can dance. It wasn't about that." He leaned down so that he could look me in the eyes. "It was just an excuse to get to hold you. I just liked feeling you there with me, you know?" I returned his gaze.

He put his arms around my waist and started dancing again.

"What are you doing?" I looked around to see if anyone was watching.

"I'm dancing with the prettiest girl I've ever seen." His face was glowing. He looked so happy. He took my hand and twirled me in circles. Suddenly it didn't matter who was watching or what anyone was thinking. Scott had wiped away all of my insecurities. I couldn't help but laugh at him; laugh with him.

"There it is…" He stopped moving to kiss me.

"I'm the luckiest guy here, you know that right?"

"Because you don't have to go to classes?"

"Because I'm with you. Maybe no one else gets that you are the most amazing person alive, but I do." He hugged me close to him.

* * * * * * * * * * * * * * * * *

"What did you think about IU?" Dad had thought by going to visit IU I would instantly change my attitude regarding college.

"It was okay, I guess." I didn't feel like elaborating.

"Well… do you think that is where you will want to go?" Dad seemed excited to hear my answer.

"I don't know, Dad. I should probably weigh all my options before making any final decisions." I smiled as I used one of his favorite phrases. Knowing I wouldn't hear any comments in return I climbed up the stairs and entered my room.

MARCH

With the early spring came the official track season. The first meet was only days away.

"You're coming right?" I begged Scott as he helped me clean the dinner dishes. That was always my hate job, especially since I was rarely there to enjoy the meal thanks to track.

"I wouldn't miss it. I can't wait to see you skunk everyone." I could tell that he was laughing at me.

We were going up against three other schools from farther north. I would have to ride the bus there, but Scott could drive me home. The rumor was that college scouts would be in attendance. It didn't really matter to me. College was still something I dreaded thinking about. However, having scouts there would mean that everyone else would be putting on their A game. I didn't want to get smoked at my first meet.

Coach Roberts had me running all the sprints for the girls' team. At times I wished that I had never committed to joining the team. Being the team's only sprinter was bringing with it a lot of pressure to win. However, I couldn't deny that I had enjoyed the running. The people were okay, too.

"Will you still love me if I come in dead last?"

"Yeah… but, I might pretend not to know you." He laughed. He continued to laugh as I slugged him in the arm. I couldn't help but notice him wince a little. I didn't have to ask why. I only let the thought cloud my mind for a moment. I didn't want him to see my reaction to his pain; a pain that he was clearly trying to hide.

"Ha Ha… You're really funny." I threw some soapy water in his face to try and break the mood.

The day of the track meet I was a mess. It was the first time that I didn't want the school day to end.

Mr. Roberts let us change into our track outfits during gym. He didn't make us run so we could save all our energy for the meet.

"You look green…" Kelly said to me as she was changing into what could only be described as the world's most horrible uniform.

The shorts we had to wear were florescent orange with a black stripe going down each side. They were very short and very tight. The shirt wasn't a shirt but rather a black tank top with a thick horizontal orange stripe going across the middle. The top was also very tight. Putting the outfit on made me feel like a slutty version of Charlie Brown. Supposedly the design of the outfit was aerodynamic. I just figured that the school hadn't had a budget that allowed for new outfits since the early 1980's.

"I feel a little green." I said as I quickly pulled on an oversized sweatshirt over my head to help cover up my uniform until the last possible second.

"Seriously, no worries. Trust me… Reason one, no one ever comes to the track meets and reason two, no one cares." I appreciated Kelly's attempt to calm me down, but it wasn't working.

"Thanks for the pep talk…" I walked out of the locker room and onto the bus. There were two buses taking the team to the match. That meant that I could sit by myself. Since I was one of the first people to board the bus I was able to get a seat in the back. I immediately took out my iPod so that I wouldn't have to worry about talking to anyone during the trip. I closed my eyes and leaned my head back on the seat. I knew it would be at least an hour before we arrived at our destination. I allowed my mind to wander.

It was no surprise that Scott was the first image I saw. Seeing him allowed my nerves to slow down. I felt a calm spread over me. I knew I would see Scott as soon as our bus arrived. He promised. My parents wouldn't be there as I hadn't told them about the meet. They just thought I had practice as usual. I didn't want them there. They would only make me feel worse than I already did. I just wanted to get the whole experience over with.

I felt the bus lurch to a stop. We were there. I took off my headphones and exited the bus. It was still chilly outside so I was allowed to keep the sweatshirt on until my events.

"Lookin' good..." There he was.

"Yeah, thanks." Even though I felt incredibly self-conscious in the outfit, Scott had seen me in much worse. "I'm going to go ahead and get a seat... I want to make sure I get front row center, I don't want to miss a thing." It was a funny joke as the stands were practically empty. There were six or so very official men with clipboards sitting in the bleachers. I assumed them to be the scouts.

I pretended to laugh, "You should really take your comedy act on the road." He gave me a bear hug and left to sit down.

The meet was scheduled such that the shortest events went first. First the boys would run, then the girls. That meant I ran second. I took off my sweatshirt as I knew I would be up shortly. I could feel the adrenaline beginning to pump throughout my body. Just because I was the fastest runner in Wabash did not mean I was the fastest here by any means. In general, Wabash was not known for having the best athletes.

It was my turn to line up. I was running against six other girls as each of the other schools had two runners for each competition. My only goal was not to come in last. I didn't want to be humiliated on my first effort. Everyone got into starting position.

Run." I was off. I could feel the heat forming between my feet and the pavement. I pushed my legs to go as fast as I knew they could. I didn't pay any attention to what was going on on either side of me. I was concentrating only on forcing my legs to continue to go. First the burning started, then I was no longer able to breathe. It didn't matter, I just kept on going. I didn't stop until I knew I was well past the finish line.

I finally allowed myself to slow down. I could feel the oxygen reentering my body as I was sure I had forgotten to breathe during the race. I looked up into the stands searching for the only face that would bring me comfort.

There he was. His smile went from one ear to the other. He was giving me the thumbs up sign.

"Great job!" Mr. Roberts said from behind me. "You creamed 'em!"

"Really? Cool..." Goal reached; I wasn't last.

I had two more events before I was finished. Both of them went the same way. I was just relieved to have them over with. As soon as I finished my last race I ran directly to where Scott was. I barely slowed down from my sprint.

"You were... fast." Scott grabbed me and twirled me around.

"I am just glad it is over. Can we go now?"

"Don't you get a medal or something?"

"I don't think so... " I found his hand and lead him over to the bus.

"Don't you want to see how the rest of the meet goes?"

"Not really..."

"Okay... we can go, but only on one condition." His smirk told me bad news was on the way. "You keep that outfit on... you look hot." His words were barely understandable as they came out along with uncontrollable laughter. We both knew that I looked ridiculous.

"Fine... but I'm changing as soon as we get back to my car!"

It seemed like the drive home took half as long as the drive there. That, of course, was because I was in good company.

Scott couldn't get over the fact that I beat everyone and I couldn't get over the fact that he was so impressed. It wasn't my mission to win, my only reason for joining track was to get away from my family.

"You really should tell your parents." Why did he have to bring it up...

"Seriously? Are we going to have this discussion again?"

"Looks like it..." I could tell Scott was getting frustrated, but so was I. We had already come to the consensus that how I chose to handle my parents was my business.

"This is so not a big deal... track is not a big deal!" How many more times was I going to have to go through this?

"You are so fast... you are crazy fast! I could barely see your legs as you were running. It is a big deal! If you were normal..." As soon as he heard the words leave his mouth he knew I was furious. I was glaring at him. The word "normal" was always one of my buttons. It was so hard for me to fit in anywhere...

"Normal? What does that mean? Quick... think of something fast, something really great to say." It wasn't often that I was this angry with Scott.

"If you were normal... If you were normal you would think this is a big deal. You would know that it's a big deal. I wouldn't have to keep telling you."

"Curing cancer, that's a big deal. Winning a Nobel prize, that's also a big deal. Winning a race at a high school track meet, not a big deal. Are we done?"

"Why can't you allow yourself to be proud about this? It's okay to think you are good at something."

"This is quickly becoming a circular conversation."

"Whatever…" Scott said under his breath while shaking his head.

Upon arriving at the high school parking lot, I jumped out of his truck and into my wagon. I was so mad I was shaking. I didn't look at him as a I drove away. I couldn't tell him everything. I hated complaining about my parents to him because comparatively, they were perfect. However, they still drove me nuts. It didn't help their cause that I knew their true feelings about Scott. How they could be so dismissive about a relationship that meant so much to me was unacceptable. I couldn't explain that to Scott. I knew that if he found out how my parents really felt that it would devastate him. I also knew that he would put on a brave face and pretend that he wasn't bothered by their opinions.

Scott was following me home. I didn't glance once into the rearview mirror. I was still too infuriated to look at him. Between him and my parents I felt like no one was listening to me, or at least not really hearing me. I didn't know if it was my inability to communicate, or his inability to understand. Either way we were suffering from a bad case of miscommunication.

I pulled in front of my house. Before getting out of the car I slipped sweatpants on over my shorts. I didn't want to have to explain the outfit to my parents. I wasn't surprised when Scott pulled up immediately after me.

"We need to put on a good show," I told him as I got out of the car.

"What?"

"I don't want them to know that we are fighting." I didn't want to tell Scott that our argument would probably make my parents very happy.

"So…let's just stop fighting. That would solve the problem, right?"

"Do you agree that you are wrong?"

"No, but I will agree that it is not my business." He took my hand as a sign of a truce.

"Fair enough." Hand in hand we walked through my front door.

* * * * * * * * * * * * * * * *

"Sid, that you?" I heard Mom call from the kitchen.

"And Scott…"

"There's food on the counter if you are hungry." Scott and I walked back to join the rest of my family.

"Did you hear yet?" As soon as Scott said the words I knew what was coming next. I could feel him move away from me as I was sure he knew he was in physical danger.

"No…" Dad said quizzically. "What should we have heard?"

"She beat 'em all. Every race…." I could've hurt him. I could've pulled his head right off of his neck.

"What do you mean?" My mom looked hurt… like there had been a party and she wasn't invited.

"No big deal… first track meet was today and I did pretty well." I was trying to play it down.

"Pretty well? That's an understatement! You should've seen her! No one even came close. I wouldn't be surprised if it's in tomorrow's paper." Why couldn't he just have let it go?

"Your first track meet? Sidney, why didn't you tell us?" There was that look again from Mom..

"You won?" Even Hallie couldn't hide her disbelief.

"When's the next match?" I could already visualize Dad sitting next to all the scouts telling them I was an Olympic champion or something.

"Next Tuesday." Thank you Scott. "I'll get a schedule for you, no problem." Scott shot me a look that told me he knew he was in trouble, but that he didn't care.

After dinner was over and the mess was cleaned up, Scott and I retreated upstairs to my room so that we could have the inevitable argument that was to be the result of his inability to keep his mouth shut.

"Was that necessary?" Scott had never so openly defied me before. I thought we were on the same team. I somehow felt betrayed and I didn't like it.

"Yes, it was. Plus, you're super cute when you're angry." Scott walked up to me and put his arms around my waist. "Did you know that your entire face turns red when you're mad?" I couldn't believe that he was trying to turn our argument into foreplay.

I didn't want to talk to him if he wasn't going to take it seriously. I pulled my books out of my book bag and started doing my homework. I was hoping that he would take it as a sign to leave.

I shook my head, "You don't get it…" I couldn't look at him. For the first time, I didn't want to look at him.

"Then explain it to me. You are the best, the absolute best and you don't want to share it with the people who care about you the most. What don't I get about that?"

"That's funny... They aren't my family. They don't know me at all. All they do is judge and play pretend. They put on a really good show; you should know that... they have you convinced." I bit my lip. I hadn't meant to say that.

"Convinced of what?"

"That they think you are worth it."

"Worth what?" His tone was becoming cold.

"It doesn't matter... I feel like I can't trust you anymore. All I asked was that you leave my parents out of it. What does it matter to you? Have I ever asked you for anything? Have I ever bothered you about your dad? Didn't I respect your wishes when you asked me to stay out of it?" I knew I had made a low blow, probably an unforgivable one at that, but it was how I felt and I no longer felt like keeping it all in.

Without a word Scott stood up and left.

* * * * * * * * * * * * * *

He didn't call. He didn't come over. His absence, not matter how sudden or brief, did not go unnoticed.

"Can I come in?" I heard my mom through my closed bedroom door.

"As if I could stop you, " I thought to myself. I slid my journal, which hadn't been used for a very long time, under my pillow. I would rip out the pages later…

Mom opened the door and slowly entered my room. She looked around as if she was looking for something, evidence maybe? For what I didn't know…

"Need something?" I just wanted to get this over with as quickly as possible.

"Are you okay?"

"Sure… I guess so."

"I know these things can be hard…" She sat uncomfortably close to me on my bed. I was literally stuck in a corner.

"What things?"

"Break ups."

"Who broke up?" I tried to keep my face steady, but I could feel the tears forming. I didn't know for sure whether or not Scott and I had broken up. Neither of us had tried, so far, to contact the other. I didn't know what was going on; however, I did know that I wasn't going to admit to a break up unless he gave me a concrete reason to do so.

"I thought… we thought… Well, it is Saturday and Scott's not here, yet you are. He left so suddenly the other night…We just assumed…."

"You assumed wrong. What is it they say about assuming things? I think it ends up turning someone into an ass." I looked her straight in the eyes as I said it. That was the first time I had ever said anything so crass to either of my parents. I wouldn't have under normal circumstances, it was just that I was reaching the extent of my limit. I couldn't handle anymore.

My mom looked at me as if I had taken her heart and crushed it between my fingers. I knew what I said was wrong and I immediately regretted it, but I wasn't ready to take it back. I wanted to sound strong and confident, the exact opposite of what I was feeling.

She got up and left. A pattern that I had been creating in my room.

"I am here if you need anything, even if it is just some company." She couldn't even look at me as she said it. I was pretty sure that she was crying. To my knowledge, that was the first time I had ever intentionally hurt her.

* * * * * * * * * * * * * * *

I half expected to see Scott at my next track meet. He never showed. He didn't show for the next four meets either. My parents, on the hand, were there along with about ten other people sitting in the stands. My mom must've bought out the entire school store as everything she was wearing was orange with WHS printed in big bold black letters. All she was missing was an oversized foam finger. Dad, as predicted, was making his way to whom he presumed to be college scouts. I was mortified. If only Scott had listened to me…

I ran my sprints without much effort. Scott's absence left me distracted. Even still, I always won all three events. I seemed to draw more attention as the season progressed than I did at the first meet. Maybe at the first match people thought it was a fluke and that winning was not going to be a consistent pattern for me. Or, maybe I simply hadn't noticed as all my energy had been focused on Scott. Either way it didn't matter. I still didn't care about winning or losing.

All I wanted to do was sit in my room and remember. If I closed my eyes I could still see him. If I tried hard enough, I could still feel him. I could taste his mouth on mine. I could feel his warm hands touching me.

What I missed the most was his smell; I couldn't find it.
Nothing I did, no matter how hard I concentrated, I
couldn't bring it back. I couldn't remember.

His absence was killing me, slowly. It was like I
didn't exist anymore. I went through all the motions of
daily life. I ran track. I did homework. I watched TV. But
none of it mattered. I didn't cry because in order to cry a
person has to feel something. I felt nothing.

APRIL

"You ran a really good race yesterday." I turned around and saw Phillip, a guy from track, standing behind me. I was surprised because we had never really talked before. He had definitely never before sought me out during school.

"Um… thanks." I had zero interest in talking with him, no matter the circumstances.

"So… a bunch of us are going out after the meet Friday. You interested? I mean, it doesn't have to be a date or anything." I could tell that Phillip was struggling to find the right words.

"Thanks... But I think I'll pass."

"Maybe some other time?" He sounded so hopeful, I felt almost guilty for being so dismissive.

"You know I have a boyfriend, right?"

"It's just that I heard..."

"You heard? What?"

"Hallie said... she said that Scott hasn't been around... I haven't seen him at the track meets lately. I thought..." I could tell that Phil knew he was entering awkward territory.

"Um... no, he's just been... busy." I tried to play it off like nothing was wrong.

"I saw him, last Friday." Phillip looked nervous.

"Okay..." So Scott was still alive, that was good news.

"With Stacy. They go to school together." I felt like I had been hit... hard. The wind had been knocked out of me. I had to grab my locker to keep from falling.

"Yeah... I knew that." I closed my locker and left. I wasn't sure how long Phillip stood there. I didn't care. Scott was dating...

Scott didn't date. That's what he told me. I couldn't breathe. The walls were spinning around me. I was dying inside and Scott was dating. Thinking about him kissing someone else. Touching someone else. I was going to get sick.

I ran into the bathroom and into a stall. I sat down and put my head between my knees. I needed to world to stop moving. I couldn't open my eyes. I knew if I did I would faint. Scott was dating....

I had to get out of here. I had to get air. I was sweating even though I was cold. My entire world was caving in around me. I didn't know how to survive without Scott.

* * * * * * * * * * * * * * * *

I skipped practice so that I could catch Hallie as soon as she got home. She wasn't there yet when I arrived. The longer I had to wait the more irate I became. My hands were shaking. I felt could feel my jaw tense. Finally I heard a car door close. I ran to the front door.

"You are telling people about me and Scott?" I confronted Hallie as soon as she walked into the entry.

"And?" Her lack of compassion didn't really surprise me.

"What business is it of yours?"

"What do you care who I tell? Besides, if I'm not mistaken, it got you a date." Did she really think that she was doing me a favor?

"So if I tell everyone at school how you enjoy puking after every meal... I mean, that might get you a date. You know, guys will think you are cheap if they know they don't have to feed you." It wasn't true, I knew it wasn't true. I just had to say something that stung. I was just so angry...

"That's not true and you know it."

"Neither is saying that Scott and I broke up. It's called creating a rumor. I am sure you are familiar with how that works."

Hallie, much like everyone else in my life, turned and ran off leaving me alone.

"What was that about?" Dad, I guess, had seen Hallie run out of the kitchen. "Your sister nearly plowed me over."

"Don't know..." I shrugged my shoulders and headed for the backdoor. I had to get out.

"No... wait." I knew it wasn't going to be that easy. "We have all been pretty tolerant around here regarding your recent... mood, shall we say? There are four people under this roof. We can't all revolve around you. Now, your mother is worried sick and I am just about done with it. He was just a boy."

I stared at him. No, I glared at him. He was done? Well, so was I. I ran out the door before he had a chance to stop me again.

Just a boy... Scott was not just a boy. He was my everything. He was kind and gentle. He was funny and strong. He was compassionate. He was my other half.

The argument seemed so long ago. What was it even about? It didn't matter. I needed him. I would swallow my pride. I had to see him. Even if he was with Stacy...

* * * * * * * * * * * * * * * *

I drove down the still familiar road. It began to rain making everything harder to see. I had to slow down considerably just to make sure I stayed on the road. I just had to make it to Scott's house, then everything would be okay. He would make everything right again. I knew he would. I had to let him see me, if he just saw me he would know that dating someone else was a mistake.

narrow. I knew I was getting close. Soon the blacktop would turn to gravel. I couldn't get there fast enough.

I wasn't sure what happened. The wagon started to pull to the right. I turned the wheel to the left in order to stay on the road. I must've overcorrected because the car started spinning out of control. I didn't know how to make it stop. I couldn't see out the windshield anymore to see what was going on. I tried slamming on the brakes, but that only seemed to make it worse. The car wouldn't stop spinning. There was no gradual slowing, no indication that this terror was almost over. I stop trying to control the situation. I covered my eyes with my hands so that I wouldn't have to watch anymore.

Without warning, the car stopped. I sat there for a moment to make certain I was okay. Nothing hurt. I could move all of my appendages. It was then time to check the damage to the wagon. We hadn't hit anything that I was aware of. Maybe I would be lucky…

Upon getting out of the car it was easy to see that I was no longer on the road; not even close. There was nothing I could do to move the car. It was stuck in the middle of a field. I was pretty sure that it was Scott's field, but I wasn't certain.

That was it… That was all I could take. I was just one person. How was I supposed to handle it all. I collapsed onto the ground next to the wagon. I could feel my body sink into the mud. I didn't care. The rain was falling so hard that it stung every time it hit my skin. It was almost a relief to feel something instead of nothing.

I couldn't cry. I didn't have it in me. Instead, I just lifted my head to the clouds with the hopes that the rain would help to wash everything away. Wash away the memories. I didn't want them anymore. I wasn't strong enough. Please, just make it all stop…

"What are you doing out here?" I could faintly hear someone yelling at me, but I couldn't see anything through the thick fog of rain.

"Sidney? That you?" I saw a figure running toward me. "You okay?" The tears found me. I saw his face and everything that I had been holding in came out at once. I couldn't pretend anymore. He just stood there, staring at me.

"You left!" I felt like I had to yell so that he could hear me through the rain. "You didn't say goodbye or anything, you just left. It was so easy for you." It was difficult to speak through the sobs. "I can't… I can't breathe." I was hyperventilating. Too much too fast.

He knelt down and took me in his arms. "Shh…" He tried to get me to calm down.

"NO!" I jumped to my feet. "It isn't that easy. You can't just 'shh' me. Where have you been?"

He stood up to meet my gaze. "The phone goes both ways."

"You're dating!" I jumped right to the purpose of my trip. "You told me that you don't date. You lied!"

"I'm not dating." He looked confused.

"They saw you… at the movies. Some girl named Stacy."

"Sidney… there's no Stacy." I so wanted to believe him.

"But they saw you…"

"Who saw me?" A smile was beginning to form on Scott's face.

"Phillip… he said…"

"Phillip? Was that before or after he asked you out?" Scott said looking quite smug.

"There's really no Stacy?" I couldn't help but feel better. The panic was leaving my body. I felt like I could breathe for the first time in weeks. He was close enough to smell. I took a deep breath so that I could fix that aroma in my mind forever. I would never again lose that scent.

"There's no Stacy." He just stood there looking at me as if he had never seen me before. He took my face in his hands. He began to study my face with his fingers, as if he thought I might not be real. "You think you are so replaceable? Expendable?"

I was glad it was still raining so that the drops could help hide my continuing tears.

"I don't work without you." I had to look away as I uttered the words. I said them so quietly I wasn't even sure if he heard.

He came so close that I could feel his breath. I could feel its warmth on my neck.

"Your smell…"

"I smell?" He laughed as he smelled himself.

"I couldn't remember…" It was like breathing for the first time. I was no longer drowning. Again, Scott had saved me; he had pulled me to the surface.

He kissed the top of my head. He continued moving downward until his mouth found mine.

Scott took his jacket off and wrapped it around me. The lining still held the warmth from his body. I could feel all the holes within me healing. It was like coming home. With him was where I belonged.

Together we walked to his truck.

"We will have to fish your car out tomorrow. Trying to do it in this weather will only make it worse. I'll drive you home."

He got no argument from me. I found my spot in his truck, right next to him in the middle. It was amazing how quickly we were able to fit back together again.

"Sidney... I'm not sure how this is going to work." His words shocked me.

I sat straight up, "What do you mean? I thought we..."

"I didn't leave that night because of what you said."

I didn't know where this was going but I was getting a strong feeling that it wasn't going to work out in my favor. I felt my lungs beginning to fight for air.

"I left because... because what you said brought back the picture I have of your face in my mind when you saw Dad. I will never allow myself to forget that again."

"I don't understand... I thought we just let it go, like it never happened."

"But it did happen, and it does happen. I don't care what he does to me. I'll take it. But if he ever hurt you… " As he spoke his face became unusually rigid, almost frighteningly so.

"I'm not scared of your dad."

"What if he would've come after you? What if I couldn't have gotten to you in time?" I thought I saw tears in his eyes.

"You left because of your dad?" This entire time I had blamed myself for being stupid. For letting my bad mood ruin the best thing that had ever happened to me. When in reality, it had nothing to do with me.

"How long do you think it would've been until something like that happened again? I can't keep you away from him forever."

"Then don't. If you are going to leave me, leave me because you hate me. Leave me because you are angry. Leave me because you don't love me anymore. Do not leave me because you think you need to protect me from something that you cannot control." I wanted to tell him that the pain he caused me was more painful than any torture that could have been brought on by his father. Bringing that up would not help matters right now. I needed to keep it to myself so that we could just get through this and move on.

"Of course I still love you… "

"Why don't we leave? We are both of age, no one could stop us… We could go anywhere, Idaho even!" It sounded perfect to me. A real life with Scott, that was all I wanted.

"Sid, I can't leave."

"Yes… I have a little money…."

"No, I can't leave. You aren't hearing me." He looked me dead-on. I knew his mind was made up before even giving the idea a chance.

"Why? You could get away from your dad… People do it all the time. We don't have to be the couple that just stays here."

"You have school."

"Graduation is only a month away. We could leave the next day… we wouldn't even have to tell anyone." I would follow Scott anywhere he wanted to go.

"I can't leave my dad."

"But… he… why do you feel you owe him so much? He certainly doesn't reciprocate."

"Sid, I don't expect you to understand. But, try to see it from his stand point. Mom died because of me. Maybe not right after I was born, but she never really recovered mentally from her pregnancy and childbirth. He sees me as the one responsible for his wife's death. So do I… He was, they were, happy before me. He didn't get… the way he is until after she was gone. I deserve whatever he feels like handing out."

I couldn't believe what I was hearing; although, it explained a lot.

"You didn't kill your mother. You didn't break your dad." I didn't know what else to say. How was I supposed to respond to the feelings he was sharing with me? "Anyway, it doesn't matter. We can work through this, right?"

"I can't promise that you won't see Dad again. I can't promise that… that you won't see… "

"I don't care. As long as you are standing next to me…"

"I wouldn't want to be anywhere else." I could hear the smile in his voice. The discussion was over. I felt at peace. I was suddenly overwhelmed with exhaustion. It occurred to me that I hadn't truly slept since Scott left that dreadful night in March. I was so tired. I couldn't keep my eyes open. I fell asleep with my head on Scott's shoulder. His arm was wrapped around me. This was where I belonged.

* * * * * * * * * * * * * * * *

When I opened my eyes we were sitting in front of my house. I wasn't sure how long we had been there.

"You are so gorgeous when you sleep." I was glad that he was there when I woke up. Otherwise I might have assumed that all that happened was just a dream. "So, prom is next week…"

"Are you asking me?"

"Well, since I won't be going with Stacy…" How he loved to torture me.

"Yes, I will go to prom with you." I reached up to him with my face and kissed his scratchy cheek.

Scott pointed to the driveway, "Your parents have company." I looked out the window. There was a big black Lincoln Continental sitting there. I didn't recognize it as belonging to any of their friends. "Let's go inside, shall we?"

Scott helped me out as I was still waking up from my nap. As we were walking up the driveway I was able to focus better on the car. On the back bumper I noticed a sticker: LSU. "NO NO NO NO!" I started screaming in my head.

"Scott, let's get out of here. There's no need to go inside. Seriously… we just figured things out, can't we just be alone today?" We had to get out of here.

"Relax… it'll be fine." Before I had a chance to protest Scott was walking through the front door.

"Scott? Hi… We weren't expecting to see you today." I had to appreciate Mom's gracious manner, but I was certain that it had more to do with the guy sitting in the living room than with Scott. "Oh my God! Sidney! Are you okay?"

I knew I looked a mess, we both did. We had clearly been soaked through and I was covered in mud.

"The wagon got stuck in the mud." I didn't want anyone to know how or why that happened.

"It's no problem, I'll pull it out tomorrow when things are drier. I'll just hook it up to the tractor." Scott was trying to sound helpful in order to help restore my parents' faith in him.

"Thanks Scott…" Dad immediately looked away from Scott and turned directly toward me. "Sid, you have company." Dad pointed to the gentleman in the living room. He was wearing a black suit with a purple and yellow striped tie. This couldn't be happening.

I should've looked at the car closer when we were still sitting in the truck. I didn't want to do this in front of Scott.

The man got up out of his chair and crossed the room to where I was. He reached out his hand to me for a hand shake.

"So, you are the girl with the golden legs."

"I'm sorry, what?" I wasn't going to make this easy. I didn't want this.

"My name is Robert LeLand. I am here on behalf of LSU." Scott took a step back. I could feel his desire to leave. I grabbed his hand before he had a chance to get too far away. "I have heard great things about you. Well, your legs actually." I rolled my eyes. I wished he would stop talking about my legs.

"Sidney, Mr. LeLand is offering you a scholarship, full tuition plus room and board if you agree to run track for them." I could tell that Mom was beside herself. Her knuckles were turning white as she forced herself to stay seated.

"We haven't seen speeds like yours for quite some time. We would love to know what your training secrets are." The scout spoke with a thick accent. It was hard to understand what he was saying at times.

"No training…" I immediately regretted admitting that running wasn't something I had to work at.

"That's… amazing." He started to speak to my parents instead of to me. "There are a number of conditions, of course. There will be a contract. Her grades will need to be kept up…. Everything will have to be written down so that we are all in agreement."

"Um. Thanks. I'm going to need to think…" I interjected. I didn't want this to go any further today. I had no intention of signing anything.

If Scott hadn't been there I could've pretended that this discussion never happened; that I never had a visitor. I wasn't going to LSU. I didn't care what the offer was.

"When are you looking to get an answer?" Dad asked while he glared at me.

"Sooner rather than later. We'll need papers signed quickly. It is already the end of April…" Mr. LeLand gave me one of his cards. "I'll look forward to hearing from you. Folks, it's been a pleasure. I'll show myself out."

I felt bad for him. He traveled so far just to talk to me. I was certain that he was used to being greeted with excitement and gratitude. My total lack of appreciation would've had to have rubbed him the wrong way. I wasn't trying to be rude, I just knew there was no way.

I was still holding onto Scott's hand. I could tell he was uncomfortable. I couldn't let this split us up, not just after we had managed to somehow, sort of, work things out.

"There is nothing to think about, young lady. This is not an offer you can refuse. You will take it!" Dad was not a man of the heart but one of the mind instead. To him, this offer was priceless. Nothing could have kept him away from a free ride to college.

I wasn't being obtuse. I was very much aware of what was being handed to me. It just wasn't worth the cost of what I would have to give up.

"Scott, tell her I'm right. She will listen to you." Dad looked at Scott and then at me.

"Last time I checked this was my life. I get to make the decisions." Everyone was going to tell me that I had to go. No one seemed to care that it wouldn't matter anyway because leaving Scott would kill me.

"I can tell that this is a family discussion… I just came by to drop of Sidney. I'll bring your car back tomorrow." Scott turned to leave.

"Wait!" I ran after him.

"We're not done talking!" Dad yelled from behind me.

"Yes we are!" I ran out to catch up with Scott.

Scott didn't turn around to face me even though he knew I was right behind him. He just kept on walking toward his truck.

"I told you we shouldn't have gone in." Scott kept walking without saying a word. "Scott… please…. Will you just stop for a second?"

He opened the driver side door and just stood there. He remained like that for several seconds before finally turning around.

"I cannot be the reason that you stay. They are handing you a ticket out of here. Take it." He turned, got in his truck, and drove away. That was the second time I had to watch him leave me.

* * * * * * * * * * * * * * * * *

I stood there on the driveway watching until I could no longer see his truck. I knew I had to go inside to face my parents, but I just wasn't ready yet. I wasn't ready yet to argue. We had been so close… So close to being perfect again.

The walk up the drive was a slow one as I knew what was waiting for me behind the door. I could hear my parents yelling. I was sure that they weren't really fighting, they were just venting to each other about me.

Dad caught a glimpse of me as I was trying to sneak up the stairway in order to avoid the confrontation.

"Do you know what you have been given? Do you know what this means?" Dad walked right at me. He ended up so close that I could smell his lunch.

"We understand what you are feeling, but you have to trust us on this…. There will be other boys." I could hear the quiver in Mom's voice. I had made her cry yet again.

"You are better off without this one anyway. You are not the same person you were. You used to be…." Dad's face was turning a dark purple as it always did when he was this livid.

"I used to be silent, Dad. That's what you liked about me. I never voiced my opinion because I didn't care about anything. Now, I have something to care about.

Something that matters.." I didn't have it in me to yell. I felt defeated. Scott's decision to leave meant that I had already lost the battle.

"That's not true... Believe it or not, your father and I were both teenagers at one point. First loves can... cloud the mind." Dad turned to sit down on the couch.

Is that what they thought this was? A first love? How I felt about Scott was so much more than that. He wasn't a crush that I would get over. He was essential. Without him... I began remembering what life had been like. It was as if parts of my body began shutting down one by one until eventually there would be nothing left. He wasn't my first love. He was my only love.

"You're taking the scholarship. It would be unforgivable if you didn't. You either take it, or you are on your own. I'm not paying for an education when I know you could have gotten one for free." The color in Dad's face was returning to normal. "I can't even believe that we are arguing about this. You should be... Do you know how many people would die for this opportunity? And the only thing you had to do to get it was run fast!"

Dad had always told Hallie and me that our options after high school were to either go to college or we would be forced to leave the house and support ourselves however we saw fit. College was a gift that my parents had always intended to provide for us. There was never a conversation about not going to school. Education was the most important tool in my parents' eyes. My dad called it the "golden key" because education could open all doors. The idea of me walking away from such an opportunity was incomprehensible.

I knew the discussion was over. I went up to my room. I just needed to be alone. I couldn't fight with anyone anymore. I was still exhausted, but I knew that, yet again, sleep would not find me.

I tried to call Scott. To no surprise, he didn't answer. I knew that I would have to see him tomorrow. He still had to bring my car back to me and then he would need a ride home. I would have to make sure it was me that was waiting for him when he arrived. I didn't want Dad to be the one offering the ride back. I knew that Dad would lecture Scott about the importance of education and encourage Scott to leave me alone. Dad would tell Scott that my decision to decline the offer would be one that I would regret for the rest of my life.

That was the first time I had ever regretted going for a hike that day in October. If I hadn't gone on that hike, I would have never met Scott. Although the idea of never experiencing his touch, his kiss, his kindness made the world stop spinning, I knew that he would have been better off if I had never entered his life.

He wasn't like me before we met. He had friends. He had a life whereas I was only living in shadows. He was happy before meeting me. I had done nothing to make his existence better. I had only caused pain and heartache.

If I had not met Scott I would be going to LSU. I would be excited about moving to Louisiana. I would not be arguing with my parents. I wouldn't care who I was leaving behind.

If I had my car, I would've left. I would've started driving without looking back. I would figure it out as I went. As it was, leaving was not an option. I had no means of transportation. I could run, but I wouldn't get very far. It was for the best, running away wasn't going to solve anything.

The only answer was to say "yes" to LSU. At least give that illusion. That would make everyone happy, except me. No more arguing… No one had to know that I still had no intention of leaving. Saying "yes" would simply buy me time to figure out a real solution.

My parents were still where I had left them. They were talking quietly, almost whispering.

"Mom? Dad?" I wasn't sure what sort of reception I would get.

They both looked up at me. Mom's eyes were red and swollen. Her face looked blotchy. It wasn't hard to guess that she had been crying.

"I'll go to LSU." Both of them looked at me as if I was lying. Surely I wasn't making this so easy. "On one condition…" They nodded as if that was what they had been expecting. "I don't want either of you to speak about Scott to me again, ever. Scott and I will only have a few months left together. I don't want them to be ruined by having to listen to your opinions. If you can agree to that, then you will watch me pack my bags in August and leave without any complaints."

"That seems like a fair agreement." Mom said while looking at Dad. They both looked as if they knew there was something behind the deal, but were willing to accept the terms anyway.

I didn't want to get involved with a discussion about how great and exciting college would be. After my terms were agreed to, I went back upstairs.

I wanted Scott to know what I had decided. I called again. I knew he wouldn't answer, but I had rehearsed a message to leave on his voicemail.

"Scott… I just wanted you to know that I will go to LSU. That doesn't mean you and I can't enjoy what time we have left…. I will see you tomorrow." With that I hung up the phone. All there was left to do was wait.

* * * * * * * * * * * * * * * * *

I had to call Kelly and ask for a ride to school as I was sure Scott wouldn't be able to bring my car back that early.

"What did you say happened to your car?" I had already told Kelly the abbreviated version of the story. I could tell that she was looking for more specific details.

"It got stuck in the mud." I didn't want to say much. I knew that any information given to Kelly would be spread around the school very quickly. Between her and Hallie, my whole life would be public knowledge before the end of first period.

"How?" She wasn't going to give up.

"I was driving…"

"To Scott's house?" She interrupted.

"Um.. Yeah." There was no sense in lying to her.

"Back together?" It wasn't surprising that Kelly's interest lay not with the well-being of my car, but instead with my love life. "Phil will be so disappointed."

"I don't know if we are back together… I'm going away in the fall so it doesn't really matter." I didn't want to tell her anything about my relationship status as I was unsure of it myself.

"Ball State?" There was only a small percentage of students from Wabash going to college. Of those that went, Ball State seemed to be the college of choice. It was close to home and it was cheap.

"Um… no… LSU, actually." So began the illusion.

"Louisiana? How did that happen?"

"Yeah, I sorta got a scholarship… track." I knew that Hallie would be telling everyone at school anyway, so there was no reason to hide anything.

"WHAT?" Kelly pulled over to the side of the road. "You're serious, aren't you?" I felt bad because I knew that Kelly was really hoping for a track scholarship herself. So far, she hadn't gotten any attention from the scouts.

"The guy came over last night. It happened really fast. We didn't sign any papers or anything… Nothing official."

"You are getting a free ride… This is your first year ever running in track. There have been, what, like, four meets? I have trained the last four years…." It wasn't hard to see that Kelly was upset.

"I am sure someone will approach you… There is still more than half the season left." I was beginning to feel a sense of guilt. I had no intention of using my scholarship. It was going to end up going to waste. Someone like Kelly, she would've given anything for the opportunity. I would hate to think what she thought if she knew my real plans.

Kelly composed herself and pulled us back onto the road. I was relieved that we were almost to school. She didn't speak the rest of the way there. We walked into the building together, but she quickly went off in the other direction.

As predicted, it didn't take long for the news to travel. I was suddenly becoming quite popular. I heard word of an article about me in the school paper. That really wasn't shocking as the paper normally had to dig hard to find anything to print.

When last period came I felt a surge of relief. I already knew that Mr. Roberts would have has running our events for practice. I was good at avoiding conversation when out on the field.

"I heard about your good news…" That was the most Mr. Roberts had ever said to me directly.

"Yeah, thanks." I headed for the locker room.

"You really are a natural, you know?" What was he getting at? He grabbed my arm, "Don't blow it." His look was intense., like, I owed it to him or something.

I shook myself free, "Sure thing…" I quickly ran in the locker room to change. There were a lot of rumors flying around about Mr. Roberts. I didn't care to be added to the list.

I was the last girl to enter the locker room thanks to Mr. Roberts.

"I heard she was going to say no." Clearly no one heard me come in.

"All for that guy, the one from Northfield… She still won't let him go even though he cheated on her." This wasn't happening, not again.

"Hallie said that when they broke up she never left her room. That she would just sit there staring at the wall. Sounds like a really great time…" I heard them all laughing.

"He's so cute… I wonder what he saw in her to begin with."

I had to sit down. I grabbed the bench to make sure I didn't collapse. He cheated? He told me that there was no Stacy. I had no reason not to trust him. Even still, hearing the rumor again shook me. Just the idea of it…

They saw me as they were leaving. The looks on their faces were those of regret. Their words weren't meant to be heard by me. Was it my fault that I was in there?

The spinning was back. So much had happened in such a short period of time. I couldn't wrap my mind around everything. Was he lying? Had he ever lied to me before? I had no way of knowing.

"Sidney?" It was Kelly. I was sure the other girls had sent her in to check on me.

"I'm okay… just dizzy."

"They are just… they don't know what they are talking about. Word got out about your scholarship and things blew up from there." I didn't care about the scholarship. That wasn't what I was worried about. "I think you scare them a little."

I looked at her sideways, "What?"

"Not in an ass-kicking way… It's just that they just don't get you. You don't talk to anyone. You aren't threatened by anyone. You're dating Superman. You have this whole mysterious thing going on. And now, on top of everything else, you are handed the most sought after possession from everyone here, a way out. But that doesn't seem to phase you either."

I still chose not to speak. Kelly was only in here to try and lure me out so Mr. Roberts wouldn't have to. I let her words glide straight through me.

"They are so jealous... they don't know what they are saying. Trust me."

"What do you know?" The words were barely a whisper. I hung my head down even lower. If I could just remember how to count to ten. I had heard that counting helped calm the nerves.

I felt bad for being short with Kelly. She was just trying to help. It wasn't her fault that my world was crashing down all around me. It wasn't her fault that Scott had lied. It wasn't her fault that I wasn't strong enough to handle it all. It was my fault, all of it.

Kelly let me just sit there without speaking. She kept looking at her watch.

"I guess we should get out there, huh?" She stood up and reached out a hand to help me up.

After gym Kelly and I walked out to the parking lot together. I still thought I needed a ride home. Although, as it turned out, I didn't.

There was that big, black, beautiful truck. That truck, to me, was better than any foreign sports car. Even better, there was Scott leaning on the front bumper. Looking at him always took my breath away from me.

"See ya later…" Kelly nudged me as she walked to her own car.

I waved goodbye to her as I walked straight into the arms I belonged to. I let myself forget everything I heard in the locker room. Instead I allowed myself to find his heart beat beneath his shirt. That sound in itself made life worth all the suffering.

He kissed the top of my head. "Ready to go fishin'?"

"I don't like fish… I'd rather think of other ways to pass the time…" I joked.

I remembered the locker room conversation during the drive to his house.

"Today was rough." I wasn't yet sure how much I wanted to tell him.

"Want to talk about it?"

"I don't know yet." I knew there were still some eggshells left to walk on before we were finally back to normal. I wasn't sure how much those shells could handle.

"Well...?"

"Did you get my message last night, about LSU?" I wasn't sure how much information he already had.

"No, I lost my cell phone somewhere in the mud yesterday. I was sort of hoping we could look for it while getting your car."

"So you are talking to me even though you didn't get the message? But yesterday you were so mad...."

"I'm not mad, Sidney. Just feeling guilty, very guilty." I guess I understood what he was getting at; although, we would have to agree to disagree on that topic.

I took a deep breath, "I'm taking the scholarship. I haven't called the guy yet, but I already told my parents. That pretty much makes it a done deal."

Scott pulled the truck over to the side of the road so that he could face me.

"Seriously?" He clearly didn't believe me.

"Yeah... seriously. Still not a big deal, okay?" I was hoping he wouldn't freak out.

"Sid... that's..." He turned away so I couldn't see his face. It was just for a second, but I could tell that he had to compose himself. "That's great." I should've been glad that the news was hard on him, but I felt horrible.

"So, back to my day... Thanks to Hallie the entire school found out in record time. Lots of attention; you know me and attention. Anyway... on top of that I heard this rumor... I am sure it is nothing, but the name 'Stacy' came up again." So much for eggshells.

The long pause before his response should've warned me. "Sidney... it was just once. I should've been honest with you..." Without thinking I jumped out of the parked truck. I started running. I didn't care where I was going; I just had to get away. I felt like every aspect of my life was falling apart. Scott, my family, college... It was like everything I touched was turning to dust. The only thing I knew to do was run.

"Sid! Wait!" I could hear him running after me. He wouldn't catch me. No one ever could; hence the scholarship. I took off through the fields. It was hard to keep my footing because the ground was so soggy. It was like running through wet sand, only thicker. It didn't matter, I just kept going. Focusing on my feet actually helped. It kept me from thinking about Scott... and Stacy.

Finally exhaustion hit. I couldn't run anymore. I didn't know if Scott was still behind me or not. I hoped not. I collapsed onto the ground. Once again I was sinking. I hoped that the Earth would continue to swallow me. No part of me wanted to continue.

I felt him behind me.

"You lied." I didn't want to look at him yet.

"It didn't mean anything."

"I don't care. You lied."

He sat down next to me. "I was so happy to see you... I didn't want to ruin it. We were going to have a second chance."

"I could've taken it. I went to see you to convince you that she wasn't the one, I was. You lied... " I knew I was repeating myself, but that was the only thought in my head. "You made me look like an idiot. How can I trust you now? You are supposed to be the one person on my side..."

"I am on your side... that's why I didn't want to tell you. I knew you were hurting."

"You weren't hurting? You pitied me?" I didn't want him if he was only with me because he felt sorry for me.

"Is that really what you think? That I'm with you because I feel sorry for you?"

"That's what it sounds like…" I just wanted the conversation to be over. I couldn't handle this, not again, and definitely not so soon.

"You don't know anything…." He muttered under his breath.

"Then tell me. Help me to understand. Please…" I hated that I was begging, but I needed to hear something comforting.

"I'm not good with words… You know that." His eyes were pleading with me to let him off the hook. I simply couldn't this time.

He stared at me for quite some time before saying anything. "You are… you are like oxygen to me. Without you…. I was dying, slowly. In front of everyone…. No one would leave me alone. People kept telling me that I was overreacting. That there were other girls. That you were just a girl…." He grabbed both of my hands. He was trembling. "No one understood. I thought if I went on one date with one girl then maybe they would just let me have some peace. It didn't work. You see, the whole time I was with her, I was with you. You were there in the seat next to me. It was your eyes that I saw when I looked at her. It was always you. And it will always be you. I couldn't pretend." He placed my hands on his chest. "This heart is yours. Do with it as you will." He kissed the palms of my hands.

"Are you lying?" I hated asking, but he lied so easily the first time.

"I have no reason to, you are leaving anyway. What good would it do to lie now?"

"I thought you wanted me to go."

"Just because I think you should go does not mean that I want you to."

"Scott, come with me." I knew his answer would be no, but I had to try.

"You know the answer to that question."

"It isn't your fault… you didn't kill her and you can't fix him." I was afraid that I might have gone over the line again.

Scott just sat there. I wished I could know his thoughts. He finally stood up. I was scared that he was going to leave me again. Instead he helped me up.

"We both know how this story is going to end. Instead of talking in circles, can we just both agree to try and make the next few months as perfect as possible?" I could tell in his voice that he was trying very hard to keep himself together. I didn't want to fight anymore, especially since I still had no intention of ever leaving unless Scott was by my side.

I placed one hand gently on each side of his face. "I love you more than life." I kissed him to hopefully let him know that I meant what I had said.

* * * * * * * * * * * * * * *

Prom was one week away. Both of our proms were on the same night. We planned to go to mine first, then his. The decision wasn't based on anything more than the flip of a coin.

I had no idea how to even go about approaching the idea of getting ready for prom. I knew it was a big deal, but it just didn't matter that much to me. It wasn't that I didn't want to go, it was just that I had already accepted the fact that I wouldn't be going.

I was sitting in my room contemplating my dilemma when Hallie came to my door, "You busy?"

"Um... not really." Hallie's presence was shocking, it could only mean bad news.

"Picked out a dress yet? For prom I mean..." Hallie was acting very fidgety. This was clearly uncharted territory for the both of us.

"Actually, no... I was just thinking about that."

"You are aware that you cannot wear jeans to prom, right?" There was that familiar sarcastic tone that I known to expect from her.

"Yes, thank you. If that is all..." I motioned toward the door. I didn't feel like volunteering myself to be the subject of one of her mocking sessions.

"I didn't mean it like that... It's just I thought I could help... "

"Seriously?" There had to be a catch.

"I know that you don't think I get it, but I do." She took a few more steps into my room. I wasn't sure if she had ever entered my room before.

"Get what?"

"I heard about what happened the other day in gym. I... um... Well, I just feel sorry that it happened like that." She started picking at her thumbs, something she always did when she was nervous.

"How was it supposed to happen? Was there a plan?" If she had plotted my self destruction, then I wasn't about to let her feel good about herself by picking out my prom dress.

"I didn't mean it like that… I guess I was just trying to fit in by handing out hot information, you know? That's the best way to stay in the circle. Anyway, I guess I just didn't think about how it would affect you."

"Since when do you care about how anything affects me?"

"Sidney, that's not fair. You are my sister. Just because it is my job to drive you crazy doesn't mean that I don't care. Watching you while you and Scott… it was hard on all of us. You are always a hermit, but this time it was like you were a zombie or something, like you had died." Hallie was closer to the truth than she knew.

"So do you already have a dress picked out?" I needed to change the subject. I couldn't think about life without Scott.

"Sort of. Can I show it to you?"

"You already bought it?"

 going to need one… bit since I won't…" Hallie's eyes welled up. I was afraid she was going to start sobbing, but she didn't. Instead she just closed her eyes, took a deep breath, and continued.

"I can't wear your prom dress. That wouldn't be right. What happened with Evan? Weren't you guys… dating or something?"

"We broke up after…" Hallie was referring to the incident on my birthday.

"I'm so sorry. I guess I should've paid more attention." How did I not notice that Hallie and Evan had broken up?

"I really just wanted to go to prom. I wasn't that into him. As it turns out, he wasn't that into me either. He is already dating someone else." Hallie didn't seem as upset as I would've expected. "I didn't come in here to analyze my relationship with Evan, I just wanted to know if you wanted to wear the dress, despite the fact that it isn't made out of denim our fleece." With that we both started laughing. I guess it wasn't hard for anyone to guess what my two favorite materials were.

"Yes, I would love to wear the dress."

Hallie ran out to fetch what I could only imagine to be the pinnacle of high school prom formal wear. I was envisioning beads, sequins, and- I shuddered at the thought- feathers. As it turned out, I couldn't have been more wrong. Hallie came back carrying what surely was a duplicate of Cinderella's ball gown. It was hard to tell if it was blue or silver. The color seemed to float between the two. It was strapless, but it had a wrap that went around the shoulders made of the same material as the dress. The bodice was tastefully fitted while the bottom half flowed all the way to the floor. It was stunning.

"I don't suppose you have any shoes to go with this? You can't wear tennis shoes either." Hallie mocked while laughing. She knew I wouldn't own anything that would compliment the dress.

"Know where I can find some glass slippers?"

"Well, they aren't glass…" She held out a pair of silver strappy heels. They were perfect.

"I don't know how to thank you for this. I…"

"If you meet any cute guys at LSU next year, make sure you tell them about your super hot little sister." I knew that she wanted me to think she was kidding, but I also knew that she wasn't. How many people was I going to let down by not going away in the fall?

"Sure thing."

Hallie agreed to help me on the big day with all my preparations as I was absolutely useless when it came to hair product and makeup. I did not, however, anticipate being woken up at 7am to let the festivities begin.

"Is it really going to take twelve hours to get me ready for a dance?" I felt like sleep right now was way more important than getting my nails done.

"This isn't a dance... this is prom!" Hallie yanked me out of bed. I was beginning to wish that I wasn't going.

Hallie and I spent the entire day doing my hair, polishing my nails, finding the exact shade of makeup to use... We went to store after store in search of just the right colors to compliment my eyes and hair while still matching the dress. We had to find earrings and other necessary accessories. I was relieved when we finally arrived back at home.

I was instructed to sit as still as possible until it was time to put on the dress. There was to be no risking of the hairdo or nicking of the fresh polish. It was torturous.

Scott was coming to get me at seven o' clock. I was allowed to put the dress on at 6:45. It was easier to do as Hallie ordered rather than try and fight her. That was the first time in her existence that she was willingly offering her help. I didn't want to ruin it. Besides, I knew that she was actually enjoying dressing me up; like I was her own personal living doll.

Scott rescued me right on time. I was still upstairs when I heard the doorbell ring. I tried to bolt downstairs as I didn't want Scott to suffer any time alone with my parents.

"Calm down, you should always make them wait." Hallie said as she was reapplying any makeup that she felt had worn off.

"Seriously… we are done here." I had let her have her fun. It was time for her to let me have mine. I slipped the shoes on and went to meet my escort.

He saw me as I slowly descended the stairs. I wasn't trying for a dramatic effect, I was trying to prevent a broken ankle.

There he was, standing in the front hall doorway. He looked so… perfect. He had put his own personal touch on his tuxedo. He wore a vest, but it was unbuttoned as well as the top two buttons of his shirt. He had chosen to go without a tie. To some he might've looked as if he had already been to prom and was getting undressed. Anyone else would've looked sloppy. Scott, however, looked gorgeous.

"I don't think I've ever seen you in a dress before…" His gaze was studying me intently. "I like it…."

I nodded my head in the direction of my parents. I wasn't sure how much of this conversation I wanted them to hear.

"Can we go now?" I pleaded with Scott.

"Not yet! I need to get some pictures first!" My mom was quick to pull the camera out of its drawer. She might've had to wipe the dust off as I couldn't remember the last time it had been used.

After about one hundred pictures were taken Scott and I were free to leave.

"You really do look amazing." I could feel my face getting hot. I was sure all that blush Hallie had put on me was no longer necessary. "I want to kiss you, but I don't want to ruin all that hard work."

"It isn't my work." I leaned over and kissed him. I didn't care about what my lip gloss looked like. All I cared about was Scott. Being with him made me forget the torture Hallie had put me through all day.

The prom wasn't being held anywhere special. The only place the school could afford was the gym. The budget only allowed for a few balloons and streamers. I was sure that the sound system was something a student brought in. Even still, everyone seemed to be loving all of it.

All of Wabash was seemingly somehow involved with the production that was prom. Both the yearbook and newspaper staff were there interviewing attendees. Even the city paper was there. It seemed ridiculous that the smelly school gym could possibly be the site for such a popular ordeal.

"It isn't right, you know?" Scott said.

"What isn't?" I watch him scrutinizing all of it.

"You in that dress… it just makes everything else look so… tacky." He wrapped his arm around my waist and pulled me to him. "You deserve so much better than this." I heard the joke, but the tone was serious.

"This isn't my dress. It belongs to Hallie, remember? So, eat your heart out now because you won't be seeing this again."

"It isn't just the dress… you are so much better than all of this." His mood was becoming much too somber for the occasion.

"This is a dance right?" I held out my hands to him. I felt a slow song coming on and I didn't want to miss the chance to hold him.

Scott followed me out to what had been designated as the dance floor. Taylor Swift's Love Song started to play. It seemed very appropriate that our first slow dance was to something country. As soon as Scott started spinning me around the dance floor nothing else in the world mattered. I felt like Cinderella. Being with him made everything possible.

"I should probably say 'hi' to Kelly." I nodded my head in the direction of a group I recognized to be made up mostly of the track team.

"I'll grab some punch and meet you over there." I reluctantly let go of Scott's hand. I hated being away from him, even if only for a moment.

I walked over to Kelly's table, "Hey there…"

"Oh hi… I didn't know you were coming…" Kelly didn't seem too excited to see me.

"Yeah, it was sort of a last minute thing."

"Great dress…"

"Hallie got it…" It was then that I noticed why Kelly was acting weird. Evan came up from behind her and put his arm around Kelly's waist. "Evan… hi…"

His look pretty much matched Kelly's, "Uh…" That was as articulate as I could tell Evan was going to get.

"No worries, Evan. She isn't at home pining away."
I didn't want him to think that Kelly was at home crying
herself to sleep over him. I didn't want to give Evan that
sort of satisfaction.

Scott walked up and stood next to me.

"Scott, you remember Evan, right?"

"Sure... he's the guy who drank away your
birthday." Scott replied while looking straight at Evan.
Scott gave me a little squeeze. I knew what he meant. So,
apparently, did Evan. Evan grabbed Kelly and walked away
giving Scott and I what I was certain Evan thought to be a
mean glare of sorts. Although, my mood wasn't going to let
anything ruin this night, including Evan's sour attitude.
"Here's your punch."

"You know, I'm not that thirsty anymore." I placed
my drink on the table and wrapped my arms around Scott's
waist. "Thank you for being wonderful." I gave him a kiss
that was short enough to be appropriate for a school dance
but long enough to get my point across.

After spending a gracious amount of time dancing
and mingling with the few friends I had, Scott and I decided
that it was time to go. We did have another prom to get to
before the night was over.

All the way out to truck Scott gave me very strange looks. "I have a surprise..." I wasn't terribly shocked by his statement.

"I'm a little afraid to ask." The truth was, I had terribly missed his surprises.

"We're not going to Northfield's prom."

"What about all your friends, I thought you were looking forward to hanging out with them?" I wasn't going to mind skipping another dance, but I was under the impression that Scott had really been looking forward to all of this.

"I just don't... I don't want to share you. I know you got all dressed up, and I hope you're not upset with me..."

"I'm not upset; although, I am very curious."

"I have something else in mind, okay?" There was a definite twinkle in his eye.

"You aren't going to tell me, are you?" I knew the answer before I asked the question. Scott shook his head. "Well then, let's go."

Scott didn't say a word the entire length of the trip. It was hard to tell, but I felt as if he was almost nervous.

"Do you mind walking? I mean, can you in those shoes?"

"I think I can manage. I've never really tried walking with heels on." The idea of going for a hike in shoes that I was certain could kill me was a little unnerving, but nothing was going to keep me from whatever it was Scott had in store for me. "I might need a little help, just to make sure I don't fall on my face."

Scott pulled the truck over to the side of the road. I knew where we were. I knew where we were headed. The trestle. Although we had been there a number of times, it was always a thrill. It was like our secret place. Nothing bad could touch us there.

The walk wasn't nearly as life-threatening as I had thought it would be. Hallie would've been proud at my ability to remain upright while walking in heels; although, my anticipation at that moment would've allowed me to walk across coals without feeling any pain.

The walk was a quiet one. Neither of us wanted to spoil the moment with words. I knew we were getting close. I didn't know what to expect. He held my hand the entire way helping me through spots where he knew the ground was uneven. When we came to the edge of the woods he walked in front of me so that he could hold back any branches that might've gotten in the way of my path.

I didn't need him to tell me when we had arrived at our destination. I could see it from a distance. It was somehow illuminated. As we got closer I could see what he had done.

"How did you have time to do all this? I mean, when?" What I was looking at was unbelievable. Nothing like this was possible in real life. He must've made a hundred luminaries out of white lunch bags and white votive candles. He had strategically placed them throughout the small area. He had created our own dance floor of sorts by outlining a small circle with the candlelight. He had lit a path all the way to the top of the trestle and across the top to the other side. In the middle of the trestle there was a blanket spread out. Wild flowers were strewn everywhere; flowers of yellows, pinks, blues, and purples. It was the most spectacular sight I had ever seen, and it was all for me.

"It didn't take me quite as long to get ready for today as it did you," he smiled. "I wanted to use white lilies... I know they are your favorite, but..." He turned his head down, he was ashamed. I knew that lilies weren't a part of his budget.

"This is perfect. I wouldn't do anything differently. I love it." No one had ever done anything even remotely close to this for me before. It was almost overwhelming. There I was standing in a Cinderella dress in the middle of a fairytale. It was the first time in my life that I actually felt like a princess.

Scott reached out his hand. Without question I took it. He led me to our own personal dance floor. He turned on the music. The music wasn't anything that anyone else would have thought special. To me it was perfect. He had made a collection of all the songs we had listened to that night so long ago at the bonfire after Homecoming. Even though some of them were fast, we still danced slowly in each other's arms. If I ever prayed for anything, I prayed for that night to never end.

Scott led to me to the top of the trestle. The lights, if possible, looked even more beautiful from up there.

I looked over my shoulder and saw Scott kneeling down on one knee on the blanket that he had spread out. He pulled out of his pocket a small, velvet, black box. My heart was racing. I felt my body heat up. He opened the box. In it sat a delicate yet beautiful diamond ring.

"I am not asking you to marry me." His voice was shaking. "I want you to have this ring as a sign of my promise to you. I promise to love you forever. I promise to be whatever it is that you need me to be. If you need me to be your partner, then I will gladly fill that roll. If you need me to be your friend, I will. When you leave, if you decide that you don't need me at all, then I will go. All I want in this world is for you to have everything you want and deserve. I know that things might get harder before they get any easier, but I promise to always be the light at the end of your tunnel.

This ring belonged to my mother. I want you to have it. I thought maybe you could wear it around you neck…" Scott pulled a gold necklace from his pocket and strung it through the ring.

"That way it is closer to my heart." I kneeled down next to him so that I could look in his beautiful eyes. "Come with me," I pleaded.

"I will always be here for you. Always. You are a part of me, like nothing I can explain. But, I can't leave." There was regret in his voice.

"I can't leave without you. I don't know how to do this without you." I hugged him. I placed my head on his chest and wrapped my arms around his broad body. I didn't want to cry. This moment was too wonderful to ruin with tears. I tried to stop them from coming, but I couldn't.

I loved him so much... this gesture, this amazing gesture, made me realize how much it would hurt both of us if I left. It wasn't just about me anymore. Neither of us could survive the separation.

"Sidney, we have 112 days left until you have to go. I intend to make each one of them as perfect as I can. In order to do that, you are going to have to stop asking that impossible question. Please..." His request was simple. I had to agree.

Scott leaned his face into mine and softly kissed my lips. He took me in his arms and pressed me close to him. There was no longer a sense of urgency, it was a simple act yet it spoke volumes. He had bound me to him. The ring I wore around my neck would be a constant reminder of what we meant to each other.

Still in each other's arms we stood up. I held tightly onto his hand. I refused to let go of him. We walked down the trestle and to the path that would lead us back down to Earth.

Walking down the path was much trickier than the walk up. I somehow managed to get my foot caught in the hem of the dress causing me to tumble down the rugged terrain. I heard the dress tear as it got caught on a root popping up from the ground. My once beautiful dress was now in shreds. My descent ended abruptly as I slammed directly into a bush forcing my face into its branches.

"Are you okay?" Scott came rushing after me as I had clearly past him on my way down the hill.

"Fine..." I mumbled.

"Are you hurt?" Scott was by my side helping me back up to my feet. I could feel my face flushing from pure embarrassment.

"No... not physically anyway." I stood up and took inventory of all the damage I had caused. I had ruined the dress, my hair, and had managed to break the heel off of one of the shoes. Yet again, Scott was witnessing me becoming a complete disaster.

"You are a lot prettier like this anyway. I much prefer your hair down." Scott said smiling as he picked flowers out of my hair. I could tell he was trying very hard not to laugh. "You are more in your natural state right now." I couldn't help but smile too. He had made a strong point.

"Can I borrow your socks? I know I won't make it all the way back to the truck trying to maneuver in what's left of these shoes."

Scott removed his shoes and generously gave me his socks. They were huge on my feet, but they would serve the purpose until I got back home.

We walked hand in hand back through the woods and into his field. We were both laughing at my expense. It was still the most perfect experience of my life. I was sad to see the truck come into view because that meant our night was almost over. All we had left was the seemingly short drive back to my front door.

Scott stopped just outside of the passenger door. "This was… I don't know how to say it."

"You don't have to, I know. Me too…." He kissed me one more time before opening the door.

Scott put the key in the ignition and turned it. Nothing happened. He tried again. Still, nothing.

"You aren't going to believe this. I think the battery is dead." Scott didn't look terribly upset about the turn of events.

"What now?"

"Mind walking back to the house? I will have to borrow Dad's car to get you back home."

"Will your dad care?" The memory of my last meeting with Mr. Andrews came flooding back.

"Not if we are very quiet…"

The walk to his house was almost as long as the walk to the trestle, just in the opposite direction. I didn't mind. It just gave us more time together. Scott's socks were becoming quite soggy, but I hardly noticed. We talked about our future together. Marriage. Kids. The farm. I could see all of it in my head. We talked about growing old together. It made four years of college seem almost doable when thinking about all the things our future held for us. I would be home every summer and during every holiday. He said he would come visit, if the truck could survive the drive.

We walked right up to the barn. I felt chills go up my arms. The last time I was here… I shuddered at the thought. Scott walked over to the keys hanging on the wall. After examining the lot he turned around empty handed.

"They must be in the house. You wait right here, okay?" With that Scott ran out into the darkness.

I wasn't wearing a watch; I had no way of knowing how much time had passed. I tried to envision Scott walking to the house, grabbing the keys, and then walking back to me. He was gone too long; too long to just grab a set of keys. What if his had dad woken up? I couldn't help but let my mind wander to the last time I had stood in this barn. What if Scott was laying on the floor bleeding? What if he needed my help? I was torn. A part of me wanted to run into the house and help Scott. Another, louder, part of me wanted to stay where I was, where I felt comparatively safe.

Scott would come after me. If he ever thought I was hurting, he would help me. I couldn't let myself think that I wasn't strong enough to do the same. I started walking toward the house. I had only been inside a few times. I was scared. I was scared that I would find Scott on the floor. I was scared that his dad would be waiting for me. Instead of counting my fears I decided to count my steps. One... two... three...

In sixteen steps I made it to the front door. I forced my hand to reach for the screen door handle. I had to will myself to pull it open. I remembered the door being very squeaky. I knew the sound would awaken the bear if he wasn't already. I stepped into the house. I looked around but didn't see anything. Everything was dark. Surely if there had been an altercation of sorts a light would be on or I would hear movement. I heard nothing. Still, I had to check everywhere. All Scott had gone for were keys. It wouldn't have taken him this long. I walked to the back of the house. Nothing. He wasn't here. He must've gone back to the barn. I ran for the front door. Nothing in me wanted to stay in this place.

"Where're you running off to?" There was that voice. It made my heart stop, but not in the familiar way in which Scott's voice did. I felt terror. I was alone in the house with Mr. Andrews.

"I'm not running. Just looking for Scott." I spoke quietly. I didn't want him to hear my fear.

He took a good look at me. He walked closer. I wanted to back up, but I was already against the wall. There was no where for me to go. He stopped. He was close enough to touch me. The room was still dark. I tried to control my breathing, but I couldn't. Count to ten... I told myself. I couldn't remember how. My entire body was shaking. I was certain only a few moments had passed, yet it felt like hours. He took another step towards me.

"So, this is why Scott spends all his time with you," Mr. Andrews said while handling the tear on my dress. He also began picking what was left of the wildflowers out of my hair.

I understood what he was getting at. "No... it isn't like that."

He continued to get closer. I could smell him. He smelled like stale beer and smoke. It was repulsive. It reminded me of the stench of a dirty gas station.

He continued to play with the tear in my dress. He put his other hand on the back of my head as to bring me closer to him.

"Don't touch me." I tried to break free of his grasp. His hands were strong. They refused to let me go.

He didn't say a word. He just looked at me. There was hate in his eyes. I wanted to let go of the fear but it was swallowing me. I didn't know how to get away from him. He put his face in my hair. I could feel him drinking in my scent. I was suddenly very aware that nothing was covering my shoulders. I felt naked.

Where was Scott? He should've noticed by now that I wasn't in the barn. I kept thinking that at any second I would see Scott in the doorway.

Mr. Andrews grabbed the top of my arm and spun me around so that my back was to him. He wrapped one arm around my waist and the other around my throat. He found the necklace. He examined the ring.

"This doesn't belong to you," he said very slowly. He held the ring in his hand, moving it between his fingers.

There was a fierceness in his voice that hadn't been there before. Seeing the necklace, seeing the ring... I heard it in his voice. He remembered what that ring was, what it had meant at one time for him. He remembered his loss. Seeing the ring ripped open a wound that had slowly begun to close. "This... doesn't... belong... to... you..." There was fire in his words. He ripped the necklace off of my neck and threw it to the ground.

I was trying to prepare myself for what was about to happen. Suddenly, I heard the noise I had been searching for, the screen door. It wasn't a loud noise, but it meant that we were no longer alone.

"You need to let her go." There was authority in Scott's voice.

"And if I don't want to?" I could see Mr. Andrews' reflection in the window. That was the first time I had ever seen him smile. It seemed as if he thought he was finally getting the revenge he had been longing for.

I heard a click. It was not a sound that I had ever heard before.

"I'm sorry Scott... I didn't know where you were." This was all because of me. If I had just stayed...

Scott wasn't looking at me, "You will let her go...
now."

Mr. Andrews slowly turned us both around. I didn't
know what scared me more, being held by Scott's father or
the gun I saw in Scott's hand.

"You don't have it in you." He was almost
laughing.

"You don't know what I have in me right now."
Scott's hand was steady. His voice didn't waiver once. I
believed him. I truly believed that at that moment Scott was
prepared to shoot his father. Scott held his stance. He was
not going to back down. His father saw it in Scott's face.

"It wasn't yours to give away," Mr. Andrews said as
he released me with a shove that sent me flying across the
room.

The back of my head landed on the corner of their
TV stand. The immediate throbbing made my vision blurry.
I heard Scott drop the gun. He ran over to me.

"I went to pull the car around... Did he hurt you?"
I shook my head no.

Behind him I saw his father, tears were in his eyes.
It was if I was outside of myself watching everything in slow
motion. Scott couldn't get to me fast enough, yet it seemed

as if he was hardly moving. I watched as Mr. Andrews picked up the gun. I wanted to yell but I couldn't find the words.

I thought I screamed but the noise I heard overpowered me. I had never before heard a gun shot. The sound was earsplitting. I saw Scott's face when the bullet reached him. His look wasn't one of pain; it was of disbelief. He reached out to me as he fell to the floor.

Time sped up as soon as he landed on me. I felt his weight on my body. Immediately after I heard another shot. I was certain it was me. I expected to feel pain but I felt nothing. There was blood everywhere; so much blood. I couldn't tell where it was coming from. I looked across the room and saw Max Andrews lying on the floor. Half of his head was gone; splattered along the back wall.

I knew I was screaming but I still couldn't hear anything.

I rolled Scott over so that I could see his face. His eyes were open. He looked at me and started to cry. I didn't know how to stop the bleeding.

"Scott, I don't know what to do…" I put my hands over his wound to try and stop the fountain of blood that was pouring out of him. "You can't die… not now, please…. Just breathe, okay? Just keep breathing. Think about our life… think about the promise you made. You promised to always be there, that you wouldn't leave me…. Just keep breathing!" I knew I was rambling but I was frantic. I couldn't bear to pull myself away from him. I knew that if I just stayed with him everything would be okay. This wasn't really happening. Less than an hour ago we were perfect. This couldn't be happening…

I had nothing… no way to call anyone. No car to take him to the hospital. I had nothing.

"Dear God, please….." I cried into his chest. I just held him. I could feel him struggling for air. I knew he wanted to say something but couldn't.

"Shhh…. You're only job right now is to keep breathing, okay? Don't try to say anything. I will be here the whole time. I won't let anything happen to you, alright?" I wouldn't let go of my illusion. He was going to be fine. People got shot and lived to talk about it all the time. Why should this be any different?

I closed his eyes. He looked so peaceful sleeping. I simply held him. I stroked his hair. I kissed his forehead. I rocked him. I held his hand. I hugged his chest. Everything was going to be fine. He was just sleeping. He would wake up. Help would come and save him; save me.

I wasn't aware when he stopped breathing. I didn't know at what time his heart stopped beating. I just sat there with him. I still couldn't leave his side. I held him in my arms. He still felt warm. Death was supposed to be cold and hard. He still felt alive. He still smelled the same. He was still Scott. My Scott. We were going to get married and have lots of kids. We were going to watch the sunset over the corn fields. We were going to have a life together. He wasn't dead. He couldn't be dead.

The light in the room began to change. The sun entered through the windows erasing shadows that had been hiding the events of the evening. I didn't look. I didn't let my gaze leave Scott. I wanted to be the first person he saw when his eyes opened. "Open.. Please, open," I kept thinking.

I didn't hear the car pull up the drive. I didn't hear the screen door open.

"Sidney?" I didn't hear my name. I didn't hear anything. Hearing something would've meant that this was real. My reality wasn't ready to change. I wasn't ready...

"Sidney, are you okay?" I refused to acknowledge the question. I just continued to hold Scott in my arms.

"Sidney, the police are here as well as an ambulance. It is time for you to let go." Never! I would never let go. My arms wound more tightly around his body.

Foreign hands were touching me. Trying to take me away.

"NO!" I broke free of their grasp and flung myself onto Scott again. I would not let go.

More hands. Forcing me away. Prying me away from the only thing that ever mattered. I struggled to release myself from the arms that were tearing me away from Scott. There were too many; too many hands.

I broke free in the other direction. I ran out the front door. I was completely oblivious to the fact that I was still wearing my shredded prom dress. There was blood covering my body. My hair was encrusted with it. My arms and face were painted with it. I didn't care.

I ran. I ran in Scott's socks across the fields. I ran faster than I had ever run in my life. I was trying to run away from whatever this was. It had to be a dream; a very bad dream. "Wake up!" I kept screaming inside my head. My legs burned. My lungs were on fire. It didn't matter, I kept going.

I ran through the woods. I ran through the bushes that Scott had so carefully pulled out of my way less than twelve hours ago.

I knew where my feet were taking me. To the only place Scott and I ever felt safe. The luminaries were still there. They had all blown out, but the memory was still fresh. The flowers all seemed to still be in their perfect places. I walked over to our dance floor. I could still feel him here. I could feel his arms around me holding me close. He was so warm...

I walked up the path to the top of the trestle. I went to the middle, where he had given me the ring. Where he had promised his life to me. This was where our future had officially started.

It all started to hit me. The realization that he wasn't coming back. The realization that I would never see his face again. I would never again feel his hand in mine. We had had our last kiss. The world was spinning out of control. I couldn't breathe. I couldn't find oxygen. I couldn't do this alone; how was I supposed to do this alone?

I started screaming. Tears began flowing down my face in uncontrollable waves. The sobs turned into massive convulsions. It wasn't fair. If only I had waited in the barn.

If only I had been too scared to walk into that house. If only…. I became dizzy. I could no longer keep my focus. It didn't matter if I fell. I didn't care. The pain was unbearable.

I felt someone's arms catch me as I started to collapse. These were weak arms. They were struggling to keep me up, keep me away from the edge.

"Dad! She's up here! Hurry!" The voice sounded familiar, but I couldn't place it. This was all still a dream, it had to be…

* * * * * * * * * * * * * * *

The memory of that night still felt like a knife going straight through me. Hallie's arms were those that caught me; those that kept me from falling off the edge. If she would only have let me fall… all the pain, all the hurt would be gone.

My legs felt like lead as I took one step out of the car. How was I going to do this? How was I supposed to face all these people? All these people who thought they knew and loved Scott. They didn't know him. They didn't know anything about him.

It was not my decision to come. My parents were in agreement that it would help me find some sort of closure.

They were insistent that my personal trauma lay not with the loss of Scott, but with the witnessing of the death. I didn't have it in me to argue with them.

The city of Wabash had to take responsibility for Scott and his father since there were no living relatives. The city thought it best to have them both cremated. That was fine with me as I knew I wouldn't be able to watch Scott being placed into the earth.

My whole family came with me to the service. It was a social event for most people, who wouldn't want to come? I was the only one there who wanted to leave. I thought I was going to be sick...

The funeral home was packed. There was a quiet noise that filled the space. As I entered the room I felt eyes on me. I was the girl who was there. I was the girl they had to pry off of Scott's dead body. I was the girl who loved him more than life.

I didn't regret any of my actions. If possible I would still be holding onto him. I would've given anything to see him, touch him, just once more. I longed for his lips. His hands. His presence was so calming... I needed him.

I had to compose myself. I couldn't lose it, not here. Hallie took my hand. It was so unexpected that I nearly fell to the ground from the flood of emotions that hit me at once. I wasn't ready. I couldn't do this. Not alone.

I looked around the room at the black suits and dresses. People were smiling and laughing. How was that possible when the world had just lost its most valuable treasure? What was the world without Scott?

The air was being sucked out of the room. No one else seemed to notice. I was getting dizzy again. I couldn't look up from the floor or else I was sure I would faint. I forced myself out of Hallie's grip. I pushed my way through the crowd. I needed air. Hallie followed me out of the room.

"What can I do?" Hallie's voice sounded scared.

I just shook my head. There was nothing she could do. This pain didn't come with a cure. I sat down on the curb and placed my head between my knees. Hallie sat down next to me and placed her head on my shoulder. That was all it took. The tears started before I had a chance to try and stop them.

MAY

It took a couple of weeks before anyone would leave me alone in the house. I didn't know why. I wasn't threatening to do anything rash. I just sat in my room all day. No music. No books. No journal. I just sat in my window seat watching in amazement as the world continued to move as if Scott was still in it.

I tried to sleep, but sleep wouldn't find me. I just laid in bed. I would close my eyes and try to find Scott, but he wasn't there. Instead, I saw blood... everywhere. I saw myself in that dress. I remembered seeing what it had looked like after it had been taken off of me. I remembered standing in the shower washing his blood out of my hair. I remembered what was left our own prom held in the woods... what was left of the luminaries blowing in the wind. I didn't want to remember. So I no longer wanted to close my eyes.

I was going to have to return to school in a week to take final exams. There just wasn't a way around it. I didn't care whether I passed or failed but my decisions were no longer my own. There was no fight left in me. I would go through the motions. I would sit at a desk and pretend to take a test that held no significance to my life.

No one understood. No one knew that all that was left of me was a hollow shell. Scott took with him all of me… There was nothing left. I had nothing. I was nothing…

Each day was the same. Mom would bring up food that she thought I would eat. I picked at it to make her feel better, but I had no appetite. Dad would try to talk to me about how I still had so much to live for and that I was so young… I didn't even pretend to listen. Hallie just left me alone; that I was grateful for.

To my astonishment time continued to pass. The day had arrived for me to go back to school. It was agreed that I could simply take my tests and leave. There was no need for me to sit through any classes that weren't testing.

Hallie rode with me to school. I was certain Mom and Dad told her she had to for fear that I wouldn't show up if left to arrive on my own.

"You can do this, you know?" Hallie's voice was soft and quiet. I knew I was scaring her with my comatose behavior.

I just looked at her. There was nothing to say. Words couldn't make this easier.

We walked together up the long walk into the school. They were staring, everyone was staring. I heard whispers and giggles. People got out of my way to let me through. Even the crowd normally positioned around my locker seemed to disperse as I approached to put my things away.

No one uttered a word to me. Even the teachers, as they passed out the tests, seemed to look the other way when nearing me. None of it hurt my feelings. The only thing I felt was empty. Being alone no longer mattered.

I left as soon as my last test had been completed. I walked straight out the door and directly to my car. I would never be entering that building again. On the first day of school I had thought that my final exit would be met with joy and relief. Instead, total apathy...

I didn't want to go home. I didn't want to talk about tests or graduation. I didn't want to talk at all.

I got in the wagon and drove. My mind didn't know where I was going. My body seemed to have made the choice for me. My hands turned the steering wheel as if on auto pilot; as if someone else was driving. Before I gave myself the opportunity to realize where I was headed I had already pulled into the parking lot. I was at the beach, my beach. My car was in the same spot that it was the day I met Scott.

I got out and walked down the path that led me to the dock where I nearly drowned. I froze when I reached the beginning of the wooden platform. I could see the hole I created when falling through the rotted wood. I remembered thinking that I was going to die. If only I had. The pain I had felt underwater was nothing when compared to what I was feeling now. If Scott had never saved me he would still be alive. He ended up sacrificing his life for mine. That didn't seem to be a fair trade.

I remembered seeing him for the first time. He looked like something sent from the heavens. He was the most perfect person I had ever seen, even then before I knew what a beautiful heart he had.

I had to go. I couldn't do this to myself. I turned around and walked back to the car.

I knew where I really wanted to go, but I was scared. I didn't know why. The worst had already happened. There was nothing left to be afraid of. I drove down the paved road until it turned to gravel. I drove through the tunnel of corn. I drove past the spot where I had lost control of my car and had gone spinning into the mud. I drove past his truck still parked along the side of the rode.

I drove up the gravel drive that led to his front door. The house that once looked so frightening now just looked haunted. There were ghosts in that house. That's what I was counting on anyway... My only reason for entering would be to hopefully feel Scott once more.

I pulled open the screen door. I took one step inside the doorway and stopped. I saw everything; relived everything. I tried to block it out but couldn't. I saw the blood on the wall from Mr. Andrews' shot to the head. The floor was still stained red. I walked to the window where I was held against my will. I turned around and faced the spot where I had landed after being pushed away. I could tell where I had been sitting because that was the only spot on the carpet that wasn't stained. That was where I held him. That was where I watched him die.

I touched the floor. I touched the place where Scott had taken his last breath. I could feel him here. I could feel his warmth. This was what I had been looking for.

I turned and walked into his room. I had only been here a few times, but it still felt familiar. Everything was as he last touched it. The sheets on the bed reflected his last night of sleep. The book on the floor held the last page he had ever read. This room was him.

I sat down on his mattress. I laid my head on his pillow. I could smell him. I could feel his arms wrapping themselves around me. This was where I belonged. For the first time in weeks I felt like I was home. I pulled his blankets over me. I closed my eyes and slept.

* * * * * * * * * * * * * * * * *

It was snowing again, but I wasn't cold. I wasn't sure where I was, but I didn't feel lost. I felt like I was waiting for something, someone. I started walking through the field. It wasn't a corn field; this field was full of wild flowers. They were tall, up to my knees at some points. I saw someone... He was walking toward me.

My heart was pounding, my pulse was racing. "It can't believe it's you…."

"I have missed you so much." Scott picked me up and spun me around. He felt so real.

"This is what I always pictured our land to look like someday. No more corn, just… natural beauty. Just like you." Even in my dreams he could make me blush.

"I can't do this without you… I'm not working without you. I don't know what I am doing."

He put his hands on my face and gently kissed me.

"You promised me forever… that you would be whatever I needed you to be. I need you to be here."

"I tried to fight it, I really did. All I wanted was to protect you, to keep you safe. I am so sorry that I failed so miserably."

"This is all my fault. If it wasn't for me you would still be here. If I hadn't left the barn… If I hadn't walked onto that dock…"

"You were the best thing that ever happened to me. I treasured every second I ever spent with you. I was looking forward to spending forever with you. I have no regrets." He looked right into my eyes. I touched his face. I could feel his skin on my hands.

"You left me alone. No one understands… I feel like I died with you."

He wrapped his arms around me and held me tightly against his body. How could something that felt this real, this wonderful, be a dream?

"Sidney, I love you. I will always love you. I wish there was something I could do to take the pain away."

"Will I get to see you again?"

"As long as you continue to look for me, I will be here. I told you that I would always be whatever you needed to me to be, remember?"

"I just need you…" I kissed him feverishly. I couldn't be sure that I would have this dream again. I didn't want to waste any opportunity I had to feel Scott again. I ran my fingers through his hair. I touched his chest, his arms… I ran my hands up and down his back. "I love you… Scott Andrews, I love you."

He searched my neck for the necklace he had given me. "Why aren't you wearing the ring?"

"Your dad pulled it off and threw it on the floor. I didn't get a chance to look for it before…" I couldn't finish the sentence. I didn't want to ruin this perfect dream with the memory of that night.

"It is still there… go get it. Wear it and it will be like I am there with you, always."

"I'm not ready to leave yet." I held onto him. I wouldn't let go this time, no one could make me.

"You need to wake up now, but I will still be here. I haven't left you. I am always walking beside you holding your hand. You aren't alone."

"But I feel alone…"

"Take the letters… read them."

"What letters?"

"I wrote to you everyday during our brief separation. I never sent them to you. They were just a way for me to feel like I still had you; a way for me to talk to you."

"Okay, I will take the letters."

"I love you Sidney. No matter what separates us, I will always love you."

There was nothing to do but hold onto on to one another. I didn't want to leave him.

* * * * * * * * * * * * * * * *

"Sidney! Wake up!"

I bolted upright. I forgot where I was. I was still with Scott. I had found him. I looked around me… I was in his room.

"Mom and Dad are going to kill me! They told me to watch out for you." Hallie was frantic.

"It was a dream…." The reality of it was sinking in, again.

"Stay here… I'm going to call home and tell them that I found you." Hallie went outside to get better reception on her cell.

The dream had been so real… what had he told me to do? I got up from his bed and walked into the main room. I searched the floor. There it was, in the far corner. There was the ring still on its broken chain. I picked it up and put it in my pocket. I would find another chain at home. There was something else he had told me to look for. I just couldn't remember.

"We need to go." Hallie yelled through the screen door. I could tell that having to enter this place had not been something she had wanted to do. I imagine that having to ask one of her friends to drive her out here didn't help matters either.

I still needed to figure out what it was that Scott had wanted me to have. It didn't matter. I wanted all of it. I wanted everything he had ever touched, ever looked at. I wanted his books, his blankets, his clothes. I wanted anything that could help bring him back to me again.

I started grabbing anything that would fit in my arms. I piled it into the wagon.

"What are you doing?" Hallie screamed at me. "We need to go, NOW!"

"Then go…. I don't care." I just kept moving.

"You can't take this stuff." Hallie was putting herself in front of me trying to stop me from continuing my efforts. "It isn't yours!"

Her words went straight through me. It didn't matter what she or her friend thought. This was something I had to do. Seeing him again, even if only in a dream, made me feel whole again.

"He is dead! His stuff won't bring him back. What are you going to do with all his crap? This won't help you!"

I got another load out to the wagon. He didn't have much; it wouldn't take many more trips into his room. I looked around determining what would be next. I grabbed the guitar. Behind it sat two boxes. I knew the box on the bottom; those were the letters his parents had written back and forth to each other during his dad's time spent in Iraq. The box on the top contained letters that I didn't recognize. I didn't have time to read them now. But something about those letters gave me a feeling of déjà vu.

I noticed that Hallie and her friend had left when I went out to load my most recent arm full of stuff. I was sure that she was on her way home to tell Mom and Dad what a lunatic I was. I should've been bothered by that thought, but I wasn't. I had a sense of hope within me that hadn't been there just hours before. The knowledge that I might be able to see him again gave life purpose once more.

I took one final look around his room. I had emptied it. There was nothing left but his mattress. I would've taken that as well if I thought I could've gotten it to fit in the wagon.

Thanks to all of Scott's belongings, my car was beginning to smell like him; the wonderful aroma that made my knees weak. Driving home I, again, passed Scott's truck. My sudden greediness told me that I wanted that as well. I didn't stop. I needed to think of a way first, a way to get the truck to start and a way to get it home. Scott loved that truck. I was certain that I could find him in there as well.

The greeting I got when I arrived home was pretty much what I had expected. I didn't even have to step out of the car before I was attacked by my parents.

"You can't bring this into the house." Dad's words were stern, but his face looked worried.

"This isn't healthy Sidney. Having all these things won't help you to forget." Mom didn't understand that I didn't want to forget. Why would I ever want to forget the most wonderful thing that had ever happened to me?

I ignored their words and began carrying his items inside and up to my room. They were close behind me the whole time.

"Why don't we call Goodwill have them come pick all this up? Just put everything in bags and leave them in the garage." I just wanted them both to leave me alone. It wasn't going in bags, nothing was going in the garage, and there was no way anything was being donated to Goodwill.

I stopped walking mid-stairway. I turned around to face them both. "Back off." I continued back up the stairs and to my room.

At that point they did leave me alone. I could hear them talking to each other in the kitchen, but as long as they weren't talking to me, I didn't care.

It took six trips to get everything into my room. I closed the door and began working my way through all of it. I put on his shirts until I was wearing several layers. I wrapped his blankets around me creating a cocoon for myself. I surrounded myself with his books. I just sat there waiting to feel something.

I noticed the unfamiliar box of letters sitting on the floor. I reached over and grabbed it. The letters were all in envelopes, but none of them were addressed. I opened up the one sitting on top.

Dear Sid,

> *Today was bad. All of my days have been bad lately. I can only guess that it's because you aren't in them. I miss you… I miss your eyes and your smile. I went to the beach today. I walked to that old dock and thanked it for introducing us. I know this is for the best, but why does it have to hurt so much? I love you.*

As far as I could tell there were more than a hundred letters in the box all addressed to me. Now I remembered, Scott had told me to find these; that I would find him in the box with the letters. I reached for the ring in my pocket. I took it off of its chain and placed it on my finger. No matter the plane of existence that Scott lived in, I was still his forever.

I didn't leave my room for days, maybe weeks. Time no longer existed for me. I had found Scott. My only reason for being was so that I could rediscover him every day. I loved him so much. Being with him, being near his belongings was the only thing I could do that made me feel real.

I sat in my cocoon and read each letter at least twice daily. Visitors tried to come in, but to no avail. I wasn't budging. This was what I had been unknowingly searching for.

* * * * * * * * * * * * * * * *

I found the field again. I saw him standing with his back to me. I walked to him reaching my arms around his waist. I held him to me tightly.

"I found you again." I was so happy.

He turned to face me. "Are you sure this is what you want?" He face looked somber.

"What do you mean? Of course this is what I want. You are all I have ever wanted." This was my dream, I was under the impression that I was in control. His reaction to my presence was not one that I would have thought up.

"All I want is for you to be happy… I don't think this is helping."

"This is the only time I am happy."

"So the only time when you are happy right now is when you are sleeping?" What was he trying to convince me of?

"No… the only time I am happy is when I am with you. Why are you doing this?"

"Because I can see that you are hurting…"

"So you think this conversation is helping that?" I didn't want to argue. I just wanted to enjoy what time left I had with him.

"You're right, I'm sorry… You found the letters?"

"Thank you… they are, they were, everything I needed to hear. You left so suddenly…"

He grabbed my hand and pulled me to him.

"My clothes look pretty good on you. You are only supposed to wear one shirt at a time… you know that, right?" I blushed. Still teasing me, as always. This was what I had wanted, not the fight.

"I cleaned your room for you, it was a disaster."

"Thanks for that. I was going to get around to doing it myself, but I sort of got delayed."

The time for words was over. He sat down in the grass and invited me to do the same. He ran his fingers across my forehead, brushing the hair away from my face. "You will never know how beautiful you are. It isn't fair to the rest of the world you know, having to compete against you."

I leaned in to kiss him. This time there wasn't a feeling of urgency. I knew I would see him again. I put my hand on his chest.

"I can still feel your heart beating... I didn't think..."

"I am still alive here, remember?" He kissed me again.

"How much longer do we have?"

"Not much, it is almost time for you to wake up."

"Why? What if I don't want to wake up?" I placed my head over his heart so I could hear the beats instead of just feeling them.

"Don't say that. There is always a reason to wake up. I will still be here when you become tired again. My entire reason for existence right now is to be here for you. I won't go anywhere unless you ask me to leave."

I was still listening to his heart as I willed myself to stay asleep.

* * * * * * * * * * * * * * * *

I heard a knock on my door. "Sidney? You awake? There's someone here to see you." It must've been someone important because it sounded like Mom was trying to act perky.

I stood up and shook off his blankets. He would always be there... I kept telling myself. It was okay to leave for now as long as I knew I could go back. I shed the extra shirts and went downstairs.

I walked in the living room and saw Mr. LeLand sitting in the same chair he sat in last time he surprised me with his presence.

"Good morning Sidney! Or, rather, afternoon..." He smiled although I could tell he wasn't necessarily here with good news.

"Yeah... hi." I put my hands in my pockets. I didn't want to shake hands again. It had been awkward last time.

"Well Sidney, I was very sorry to hear about your loss and, well, the way in which it happened." I just stared at him. I wasn't going to contribute anything to the conversation if this was what he came here to talk about. He just stood there waiting for me to say something, anything. "Yes, well... I understand that you weren't able to make it through the last month of school due to..." He made some sort of hand gesture that, I guessed, was supposed to indicate I had gone crazy or something. "I am just here to make sure that you will be ready come August to attend LSU, get honor roll grades, and run as fast as you can to score us some track trophies."

"She will be there." Of course Dad felt it was his job to answer a question directed to me.

"Sidney, is that the case?" Mr. LeLand again asked me, not Dad, for an answer.

I nodded my head yes. "That is still the plan."

"Excellent! Well now, if you could just sign a few papers for me, then I will get out of your way." His "few papers" looked like a book. I felt like I was signing my life over to the university. I was, for the first time, happy to do it. There was nothing for me in Wabash and now it looked like Scott was going to be able to go with me after all.

Mom and Dad were elated to watch me sign the papers. I was hoping that it would also give them a reason to take a few steps back and leave me alone.   Hopefully my decision to leave would let them believe that I was okay.

JUNE

It was time to get the truck. Scott had said that the battery was dead. I decided to call Kelly.

"Hello?" I hadn't spoken to Kelly since before prom. I felt strange calling her.

"Um... Kelly? It's Sidney... Are you busy?" It was amazing how forgiving Kelly was despite my recent treatment of her. She agreed to come pick me up with jumper cables in tow.

I didn't wait for her to pull into the driveway. I saw her car pull into the neighborhood so I darted out the door to meet her in the street.

"Thanks for coming so fast. I really do appreciate it."

"You just caught me on a good day. Do you even know how to jump start a car?" Kelly's tone indicated that she was doubtful as to the success of our project.

"I watched Dad do it once. It didn't too look hard. I am sure we can figure it out."

"Here's hoping anyway... So, I haven't really talked to you since... well, it's been awhile. I'm glad to see you outside of your house."

This was why I had been reluctant to talk to anyone. I didn't want to talk about Scott or how I was doing. I just wanted to... be.

"Yeah, it's been awhile. You started getting ready for college yet?" I was hoping that the change in subject would clue Kelly in to the fact that I wasn't ready yet to talk about anything having to do with Scott.

"Sure! I can't believe that in less than ten weeks I am out! You still planning on going to LSU?"

"Signed some papers yesterday. Looks like it is a done deal. Where are you going again?"

"Ball State, along with everyone else. Although I have to admit that it will be nice knowing some people there." I chuckled to myself. That was the exact opposite thing I was thinking about college. I wanted to go to a place where no one knew me. It was going to be nice to be surrounded by strangers.

The truck was still right where Scott had left it. A part of me was afraid that it might've gotten towed or something. I should've known better... Kelly arranged her car so that they were facing each other.

"Am I supposed to keep my car running while you do this?" I barely heard Kelly's question as my concentration was focused on looking for a latch or something that would let me open the hood of Scott's truck. With effort I finally found it.

"Um... I think that I am supposed to connect the cars first. Then you start up your engine." I really didn't know that for sure, but I didn't want to risk electrocuting myself either which I considered to be a definite possibility if Kelly's car was still running.

"Well... just do your thing." Kelly got back in her car. I looked over my shoulder and saw her talking with someone on the phone. I was sure she could tell that my only interest right now was getting this truck working again.

After I had placed the jumper cables where I thought they needed to go, I gave Kelly a thumbs-up sign. I was hoping that she would take that as a sign to start her engine. Thankfully she did. "Please let this work," I whispered to myself. I turned the key still left in the ignition. Nothing happened. "Scott... please let this work." I turned the key. I heard the engine fighting for life. "Come on... you can do it." Miraculously the engine turned over. I let both cars continue to run connected for awhile. I decided that it couldn't hurt anything.

I was sitting in Scott's seat. I closed my eyes. I could see him here. I pictured him driving me to the bonfire; telling me to scoot over. I pictured him laying in my lap after gluing his body back together. I pictured him driving us to the special prom that he had created just for me. He was here. He was with me in this truck.

"So... you got it running..." Kelly walked up to the driver side window.

"Yeah... thank you so much!" I did feel bad for taking advantage of her kindness. I hoped that someday she would understand.

"Um... if you don't mind, I'm going to take off. You're okay with the truck, right?"

I got out to remove the cables so that Kelly wasn't trapped here with me anymore. "Thanks again... really."

Before she left Kelly gave me a really big hug. Just the act of being in contact with another person almost made me lose it. I didn't want that to happen in front of her. Not after all she had already done to help out.

I watched her car drive away. I would miss her. Kelly had always been there when I needed someone and she never once asked me for anything.

I knew it was time to head home, I just wished that it wasn't. I was going to drive as slowly as possible so that I could enjoy being with Scott that much longer.

Surprisingly no one was waiting for me when I got home. I had anticipated being attacked by Mom and Dad with a million questions as to where I had been and what I had been doing. I walked in the kitchen only to find a note on the counter. They had gone out for food. Perfect.

The only item on my agenda was to recreate my cocoon and reread all the letters Scott had written to me. I took the steps two at a time. I couldn't get to my door fast enough.

Something was wrong. I looked in my room. Everything, his socks, his shirts, his blankets… They were folded neatly in piles on my bed. I knew that wasn't where I had left them. I picked up one of the blankets. It smelled like fabric softener. I went through all the items. Everything smelled like fabric softener. She had washed all of it. Nothing smelled like him anymore.

I couldn't get past the horror. He was gone. These weren't his anymore. These were just some dead guy's stuff. What had she done? Why would she do this? I fell to the ground. All the feelings of hope and contentment that had started to rebuild within me were gone. How was I going to find him now?

There were no words to express the anger I felt towards my mother. I was certain she was the culprit. She probably couldn't get past the idea of me snuggling up to his dirty sheets and sweatshirts. It was her nature to keep everything sterile. I felt like I was losing him again.

I still had his letters and his books, but they weren't the same. I took his letters and went back out to the truck. I laid down across the seats. He was here. I knew he was here. He sat in this truck. He loved this truck. I clung to the box of letters like it was a favorite pillow. I shut my eyes. It was going to be difficult to find sleep now, but I had to. I had to see him, even if just once more.

I didn't move. I tried to calm my body down so that I would be able to relax. I don't know how long it took to finally fall asleep. I just started counting so that I wouldn't think about anything. 1...2...3...4...50...70...112...

* * * * * * * * * * * * * * * *

This place was so peaceful. It was like coming home. Scott saw me and starting running in my direction. Without saying anything he grabbed me and lifted me off the ground. I couldn't help but smile when I was with him. His joy was contagious.

"I feel like it's Christmas morning every time I see you."

"Scott... it is going to get harder. Mom ruined everything."

"What did she ruin?"

"She washed all of your stuff. Your smell... it's gone."

"Isn't that a good thing? I would think that stuff smelled pretty bad." Scott was mocking my bad news.

"Your smell... it's what tells me that you are real, that you are still with me. Without it, I feel lost. Like I've lost you again." I wanted him to take this seriously. I needed to know how else to get to him if not with his things.

"You don't need my old blankets and shirts to find me. I am always here."

"Doesn't feel like it."

Scott was silent for a few moments. He clearly had something on his mind but was afraid to tell me.

"I think you need me to be something different now, but are afraid to admit it."

"Scott, this is my dream. I don't want to discuss such things. This is the only time I feel whole. Please, don't take this from me." I hated having to beg, but I just wanted to hold him.

"Okay… but think about what I said." I refused to acknowledge what he said. It was stupid. Of course nothing had changed. I was his eternally. "Thanks for saving the truck."

"Can we not talk anymore? I just want to enjoy you." I sat down in the grass and pulled him down with me. I moved so that I was as close to him as any person could be. I just wanted to feel him next to me. I didn't want to talk anymore about what I needed, or how I was doing. I just wanted to pretend that everything was okay; that nothing horrible had ever happened. Why couldn't we do that?

I placed my head on his shoulder. He seemed to sense what I wanted. He allowed me to stay there in silence until I woke up.

* * * * * * * * * * * * * * * *

The headlights from my parents' car was what brought me back from my dream. I was forced to remember what my mother had done. I didn't want to fight with her about it. She couldn't take it back.

I sat in the truck long after I watched my family go into the house. They didn't seem to notice the truck or the fact that I was in it. Maybe they had seen me but decided to let it go since I had committed to leaving in the fall. Either way, I was relieved to not have to be on guard immediately after waking from my talk with Scott.

Why did he think I wouldn't want him around anymore? He was the only part of my life that ever mattered. That hadn't changed. I didn't want to think about it anymore. They were just dreams. I knew it wasn't really Scott talking to me, but still, why would he say something so, in my opinion, hurtful? Did he want me to let him go?

I went inside the house and directly up to my room. I knew my parents saw me, but they didn't stop me. I took that as a good sign. I looked on my bed at Scott's things. They were just things... blankets, shoes, shirts.... They weren't Scott. Having them in my room wasn't going to bring him back. Nothing was going to bring him back. He was gone.

My whole life recently had been dedicated to reliving every experience I ever had with him. He was my reason for everything. How was I supposed to forget? How was I supposed to heal if I didn't? Was there some sort of medium that I was supposed to find?

I felt it... the pain hit. I had to let him go. I didn't want to. I didn't want to ever let him go. He was the most perfect person I had ever met. I loved him. I loved him so much. I cradled him as he took his last breath. How was I supposed to push that aside? He rescued me from myself. He helped me discover who I wanted to be. I saw my life with him. I saw our children. We would've been so happy together.

That was a future that I would never know. I had to mourn its loss as well as the loss of Scott. I just didn't know how.

I looked around the rest of my room. Letters were scattered all over the floor. His books were in piles on my dresser. His guitar, the one he never learned how to play, sat in its case along the wall. I picked up the letters and put them back in their box. These were mine. I would keep them.

Slowly I walked down the stairs into the family room where I saw my parents watching TV.

"Mom?" I couldn't help the tears from starting. "I think I am ready for Goodwill now."

I didn't wait for their reaction. I went to the kitchen and grabbed some trash bags and empty boxes. I took them with me upstairs.

It hurt packing up his belongings. It was like admitting defeat to a battle that I had been fighting for a very long time. I slowly placed each book in one of the boxes. It became increasingly difficult to pack as my tears blurred my vision. As the boxes filled up I placed them in the hallway as I knew I couldn't look at them in my room. I put all but one blanket in a trash bag. I also kept the sweatshirt he wore to the Homecoming game. That one was his favorite. All the others went into bags.

All I had left was the truck, the letters, one blanket, and one shirt. Everything else was going to be taken away. I asked Mom to take care of that part. I couldn't be there when they came to take it away.

* * * * * * * * * * * * * * * * *

"I cleaned up your stuff today. I mean, I packed it away and donated it."

"Thank you."

"Why are you thanking me? I thought you would be angry with me…"

"It wasn't doing you any good having all that stuff in your room." Scott didn't look the same. His smile was gone. His eyes didn't have their sparkle.

"Are you okay?"

"You need to tell me something. It is going to be hard for the both of us… I just remember this feeling… " He couldn't look at me.

"Do you remember when you took me to that bonfire and I got marshmallow all over my face?"

"I knew I loved you at that very moment. You were the prettiest girl I had ever seen, even covered in goo."

"That was probably one of the best nights of my life."

"Me too." Scott turned so that I could see his face. There were tears in his eyes. He was right; this was going to be hard on both of us.

"Scott, I love you so much. There was nothing I wanted more than to spend every possible moment with you. Without you... "I didn't know how to go on. I had to remind myself why I was doing this. "It's just that, you aren't here anymore. I've been searching for a way to get you back, but there isn't one. I can't keep trying."

"I know Sidney."

"Scott, you are dead. I watched you die in my arms. I saw your father shoot you from behind. I will never be able to truly see you again. It is time for me to say goodbye." I could barely speak. It was like losing him all over again. This was the only way I knew how to pick up what was left of my life and somehow put the pieces back together. I had to admit that he was gone.

He put his arms around me. He had known this was coming. He saw it before I did. We just stood there, in our field, holding each other.

I looked into his face. "I love you Scott Andrews," and then I took a step back and I let go.

* * * * * * * * * * * * * * * *

I woke up crying. My body felt like it was covered with a lead blanket. Even still, I felt like a burden had been lifted. I had said goodbye. I had given myself the closure that I had been yearning for.

I looked at my left hand. There in front of me was the ring that Scott had given me as a symbol of our future together. I spun it around my ring finger. I loved that ring. Slowly I slipped it off of my finger. I walked it over to my jewelry box. I opened the lid and placed the ring inside.

Scott had been a gift. His presence was nothing less than a miracle. He changed who I was. He created a confident, capable person. Without him I would still be sitting in the corner in the back of the room. But it was time to allow myself to move forward. It would take all the strength I had, but I could do it. That is what Scott would want from me, for me.

JULY

My eyelids felt like lead. They didn't want to open. I could already tell that it was going to be one of those days... Some days were easier than others. The easy days were the ones that saw a smile cross my face. Those were the days that I was able to leave my room, once I even tried leaving the house. Today wasn't going to be one of those days...

I made myself sit up. I wasn't going to allow my body to remain in bed all day. Staying in bed only made things worse. Letting myself regress wasn't going to help the healing. No matter how hard it was I forced myself to go through a daily routine. I woke up and got ready for the day. I made myself take a shower. I made myself get dressed. I had to. Some days it felt as if I had to force one leg in front of the other in order to move. Other days the pattern was more automatic.

Simply existing had become easier. I no longer had to remind myself to breathe or eat. My body was allowing itself to remain alive. I didn't feel as if I was shutting down anymore. The physical pain was gradually disappearing. It was the longing, the emotional pain that I was still struggling with. There were days when all I wanted was to feel him. Those were the days when I had to let myself put on his sweatshirt and wrap myself in his blanket. Those were the days that I let myself read his letters. Somehow that seemed to help dull the pain.

The easier days weren't spent filled with a longing, but more of an appreciation of what he had been; a gift. I let myself remember what a treasure he was. I couldn't help but laugh when I saw a bag of marshmallows in the pantry. That was a good day.

Today was not going to be one of the good days. I could feel it within me, growing. The pain was reaching out through my fingers. I didn't know what caused it to be so real some days and not on others. If I knew the answer to that I would've tried to find a solution. I felt the weight on my chest. I felt the tears rising up within me. I tried to swallow them, but couldn't. I sat in my bed and cried. I didn't watch the clock to see how long I let it go on. I had to let it out no matter the duration. Hopefully if I let it all out now the pain would subside throughout the rest of the day.

I knew he was still there. He would always be there. If I asked him to reappear he would. But I couldn't. I couldn't ask for that. I didn't want to live the rest of my life with a ghost. All I needed was time. Time would heal me.

As the tears subsided I made my way to the bathroom. I got into the shower knowing that it would help hide the evidence of my waking experience. I didn't want my parents knowing what I had already gone through so early in the day.

I hadn't talked to Mom or Dad about any of it. We never discussed any part of Scott's existence, dead or alive. I never told them what I saw. I never told them how much it hurt. I didn't have to. They didn't press me for details. After getting rid of Scott's things they pretty much left me alone. I never ventured far from my room. There was the occasional trip to the kitchen, but my legs never went much further than that. There was one really good day when I tried to go running, but I barely got a block away from the house before having to turn around. The outside world held no interest to me without Scott in it.

I knew that I had to eventually leave the house, I just didn't know how. I was terrified. I was all alone. There was no longer anyone holding my hand. I had asked Scott to leave. I had to do it on my own... I didn't know how to ask for help.

I heard Mom in the kitchen. I could do this... I could reach out to her. I could let her in...

I took several deep breaths. I counted to ten. I left my room and went downstairs.

"Mom?" My voice was quiet. She looked up from the mixing bowl. I saw in her face the hurt that I had caused her. I knew that my mourning for Scott had been hard on the whole family.

"You hungry? I'm making muffins." She was trying so hard to make things okay in her own way.

"Sure... that'd be great." I didn't want a muffin, but I knew the gesture symbolized more than just breakfast. "I was wondering... I'm going to need stuff..." This was going to be hard. I was struggling for words. Mom just stared at me, hopeful. "I mean, for college. I'm leaving soon."

"Of course." I saw a smile cross Mom's face. I could tell that my request was taken as a very good sign.

"I don't know what to get… where…" I stared at the counter while speaking. I couldn't look at her. I felt my face turning red. The tears were coming again. I didn't know if I would be able to stop them.

"We'll figure it out." She walked closer to me.

"Can we go today? Just the two of us?" Hallie had been okay the past few weeks, but I didn't want my first real public appearance to include her.

"Sounds perfect." Mom just stood there for a few moments before returning to her muffins.

"Mom?" She looked up at me. "He wasn't just a boy…" There they were, the tears.

She came to me and put her arm over my shoulder. "I know." I couldn't help it. I crumbled. For the first time since I was a little girl I let my mom hold me while I cried in her arms. There was nothing I could do to stop it. I allowed myself to open up to her. Maybe it wasn't with words, but I let her in. I let her see the pain that I was trying to keep inside.

"Sidney, we love you… so much." Her words were few but powerful.

"I don't know how… I don't know how to get better. I want to get better."

Mom didn't say anything. She just continued to hold me. That was all I wanted. I didn't want words of advice. I just wanted to know that I wasn't alone.

* * * * * * * * * * * * * * * *

I stood there staring at the road in front of me. I was leaving for LSU in three weeks. How was I going to travel more than 900 miles if I couldn't even go a mile away from my house? I had to do this, it was no longer an option.

I placed one foot in front of the other until I was running. I closed my eyes and felt the wind on my face. It was a comforting feeling. I pumped my arms faster forcing my feet to go. A familiar feeling rushed through me. It felt good. I ran. I didn't think about anything. My mind was blank for the first time in months. I concentrated on breathing, on moving.

Before I knew it I was running as fast as I could. I could feel the burn in my legs. I could feel my heart pumping faster and harder. The heat radiated throughout my body. I felt alive. I felt exhilarated.

That was when I knew I was going to be okay.

AUGUST

"Are you sure you want to drive all the way there by yourself?" Mom asked as she followed me one last time out to the truck.

"Yeah… I'm sure." The drive down was going to be long, but I was looking forward to it. I threw the last bag into the back of the truck.

"Are you sure this thing will get you all the way there?" Dad was concerned that I had chosen to drive the truck verses the wagon to Louisiana. Hallie was even more so because that meant that she was stuck with the wagon. If I had taken the wagon, then there would've been hope for Hallie on getting a new car; or at least a different car.

"I have no doubt." I had known since getting the truck that it would be going with me to college. I hadn't required much, but I needed that truck. Even though things were getting a lot easier, the truck still provided a comfort that nothing else could.

"Is your cell phone charged? Do you have all your maps?"

"Yes Mom... I will be fine. If I need anything, or if something happens I promise to call."

"You will call on the way?" Considering how much they had wanted me to leave, it was almost humorous listening to their list of worries.

"Absolutely." I started handing out my farewell hugs. It was time.

I got into the truck, in Scott's seat, and turned the ignition. I pulled out of the driveway and onto the street. I watched in the rearview mirror as my house faded away into nothing.

Once I knew my parents could no longer see me, I changed course. I had to say goodbye one more time. I drove down the familiar road to the point where the pavement stopped and the gravel started. I turned down the long drive until I reached the small house that had contained all of my life within its four, weak walls. I stopped the truck. I got out and walked up to the front door. I ran my fingers over the screen door. It was hard to imagine that the flimsy door was still able to hold on after everything that had happened within the house. I pictured all the police officers walking in and out. The coroners… I had to shut my eyes. I didn't want to think past that. I wasn't here to relive anything, I was simply here to say goodbye.

I opened the door and slowly walked inside. Everything was exactly as I had left it the last time I had entered this place. The ghosts that lived here didn't disturb the material items.

I walked into Scott's room. I felt a warmness rush through me. I wanted to succumb to it, but I couldn't allow myself to do that. I couldn't let myself regress to that point again.

"I'm leaving Scott. I am doing what you would want me to do." I almost expected to hear a response. "I will miss you…" I felt the familiar burning of tears well up into my eyes. I wiped them away with my sleeve. "I already miss you." I closed my eyes and imagined the hug that Scott would have given me upon saying our goodbyes to each other if he had still been there; if nothing had ever happened.

I walked out and got back into the truck. I turned on the radio. I no longer minded the Bluegrass Country. Hearing it put a smile on my face. I drove back down the drive to the gravel road. I followed the gravel road until it met the pavement. Then, I officially began my new journey.

Made in the USA
Lexington, KY
15 November 2010